CHRISTMAS
CRISIS
IN
Chancey

CHRISTMAS CRISIS IN *Chancey*

a novella

KAY DEW SHOSTAK

Kay Dew Shostak

To Susan—
one of the
merriest
people I
know! ♡ Kay

ISBN: 978-0-9991064-5-7

SOUTHERN FICTION: Christmas Novella / Small Town Christmas / Southern Fiction / Holiday Novella / Holiday Story / Southern Christmas / Christmas Book

Text Layout and Cover Design by Roseanna White Designs
Cover Images from www.Shutterstock.com

Published by August South Publishing. You may contact the publisher at:
AugustSouthPublishing@gmail.com

If this is your first visit to Chancey, welcome!

This novella is a perfect way to visit. You won't find out anything that will ruin any surprise in the Chancey Books series, which will continue with Book Seven in Spring 2019.

If you're already familiar with Chancey, welcome back! I hope you'll enjoy this peek at one day in our favorite fictional town. A day on which Missus has announced there is a—

Christmas Crisis in Chancey.

Merry Christmas from the Shostak Family.
May it be a season of fewer meetings and more meaning.

CHAPTER 1

"Because if I've learned anything from living in Chancey, Georgia, as painful as a meeting called by Missus can be, *not* attending a meeting called by Missus has longer-lasting, and much more painful, repercussions." I try a little bravado, forcing a smile on my face and cheer in my voice. "Carolina Jessup will be there with bells—wait—jingle bells on." Even making a holiday joke is hard this early on such a gray day. My whole body sighs as I look out at the cold rain falling this Monday morning after Thanksgiving.

My seventeen-year-old daughter Savannah sniffs as she flips a swag of dark hair back over her shoulder. She lifts her knockoff designer purse from the kitchen table where she's seated. "I can't wait until I'm an adult. Nobody's going to make me go to a meeting I don't want to go to, especially when there's something important to take care of, like having an internet connection." She unfolds from her chair and slips her purse strap over her shoulder.

Aww, isn't that cute? I'd tell her how it really is being an adult, but she wouldn't believe me. Did you believe those mean adults who tried to tell you the truth when *you* were seventeen? I ignore her words and point with my eyes at the cereal bowl she seems ready to leave on the table for the maid to pick up.

Oh, yeah, we Jessups don't have a maid. Just a bed and breakfast with three guest rooms, our family of five, two jobs, a bookstore, and a partridge in a pear tree— no, scratch that, it's a squirrel living in our attic. Or so I've been told. The resident squirrel is apparently why our internet is down again.

"We better have internet by the time I get home tonight, that's all I'm saying," Savannah explains with another hair flip at the sink. "Can't believe it was messed up this whole break. Almost makes me glad to be going back to school."

"We're not having turkey again tonight, are we?"

her younger brother Bryan asks as he barrels into the kitchen. He can't weigh more than a hundred and thirty pounds, but like freshmen boys do, he takes up so much space. His arms don't appear to be under his control. Lord knows his body odor isn't. Wait...

"Ewww, what is that smell?" Savannah says, backing up against the sink.

For once, I have to agree with my daughter. "Bryan, seriously, you're not supposed to use the entire can!" I've heard horror stories of boys with body spray, but this is my first up-close encounter. Apparently his body odor *is* now under his control.

When he storms around to leave the kitchen in disgust, his backpack brushes his sister, causing her to scream like he cut off some important appendage. His other arm smacks a half-full cup of coffee off the counter, but luckily it dumps into the sink instead of the floor. Which means another scream from his sister as it splashes her light blue, long-sleeved shirt.

"Y'all are making a meeting with Missus look fun!" I yell, and lo and behold, I hit the mothering mother lode.

Both of them roll their eyes at me, at the same time, as they push past me and leave me alone in the kitchen.

Savannah rushes up the stairs shouting about being late because she has to change shirts. Meanwhile, Bryan stands looking out the front window at the rain and eating a granola bar he'd grabbed off the kitchen table. Between chews, with his mouth full, he asks me, "So you're getting the internet fixed today?"

"I have a meeting this morning, but then I'll try. You know nothing in Chancey moves fast, and seems to me the Monday after Thanksgiving could be worse than normal." In the Atlanta suburbs where we used to live, things were less personal, more removed and businesslike. I didn't know the people who fixed my car or my air conditioner or our internet, and I liked it that way. No, I *loved* it that way.

Here, in our small town of Chancey in the Georgia mountains, everyone "knows a guy." You can't get anything fixed, or even looked at, without a long discussion of how they remember who used to live in this house or how they know the person who recommended them to you. And you must have these interminable, intimate conversations because they are auditioning to become your "guy" so when you say to people, "I know a guy," you mean them.

Savannah comes stomping back down the stairs, and at the door she stops, lifts her chin, and just stares at her brother. He stares back. She looks at me and huffs in frustration, then says as she jerks open the front door, "I'm giving you a ride to school, least you could do is open the door for me!"

Bryan slides his eyes at me and shrugs. I shrug back. Living with a teenage girl is a constant reminder that you are stupid and don't know anything. You do a lot of shrugging.

When they leave, the house is empty. Our oldest, Will, is in class already at the local college, and my husband, Jackson, left before dawn for a construction site south of Atlanta. He's a civil engineer concentrating on railroads. He chose that field because he really likes trains, even in his spare time. The technical description for folks like him is "railfan." I'm not joking, that's a real term. A real thing. So real we opened a bed and breakfast for railfans because we live beside a big railroad bridge over the wide river that curves around the bluff our house sits on.

Years ago, when the railroad bridge needed to be replaced, the townspeople of Chancey petitioned the railroad to leave the old bridge and turn it into a walking bridge. Now it is a paved walkway with wrought iron railings and old-fashioned lights. Even I have to admit it is pretty impressive to be out in the middle of the river as a huge train with several locomotives roars by, pulling dozens of loaded cars behind it.

The three guest rooms in the B&B are railroad-themed. The sunny and bright Orange Blossom Special Room has lots of greenery and its own CD featuring all the versions of the famous song we could find (including Johnny Cash's, my favorite!). The cozy, soft-gray Chessie Room features lots of pictures of the adorable Chessie kittens, which were used in 1930s advertisements for that line. Finally, the stately Southern Crescent Room uses the rich greens and golds, along with polished wood, of the luxurious cars that once ran from New York to New Orleans.

After the long holiday weekend, though, the house

is free of B&B guests and turned upside down. I'm grumpy from too much food and too much family. As much as I hate Jackson working out of town, I was actually ready for him to hit the road this morning after we had coffee. I would love to snuggle up here in this chair by the front window and watch it rain, but alas, Missus has called an emergency Christmas meeting at Ruby's Café downtown this morning.

Shermania Cogdill Bedwell (Missus) got her given name because there is some clause in her family's will that says unless your name somehow pays homage to William Tecumseh Sherman, the most hated man in the South after the Civil War, then you can inherit not one red cent. Not one! Apparently on his March to the Sea, where he ripped the heart out of Georgia along with the state's will to keep fighting, he took over the Cogdill family home for his temporary headquarters. Shermania's great-great-grandmother (or something like that) was a teenager and fell in love with him. She's the one that set up the silly inheritance requirement. One thing I have noticed, however, is they all seem to find a way to use the Sherman or the Tecumseh. Why don't they use the much more normal William in their names? Nobody ever said Southerners don't like their drama right out in the open for everyone to see—and talk about.

Anyway, once Shermania married and became Mrs. Francis Marion Bedwell, she renamed herself Missus. Missus believes it is her duty, her God-given duty, to boss Chancey around, and consequently everyone who lives here. In fact, she called this morning's meeting just yesterday. Actually went to the area churches and during each one's Sunday morning service stood up and called the citizenry to arms.

Okay, so she just called us to a meeting, but it felt bigger.

Really seems like there were torches.

Chapter 2

"What fool TV weather guy mentioned snow? I'd like to strangle him with his own microphone cord," Ruby says by way of welcome as I come into her café.

She's standing beside the front door, her elbows pointed out like bent tent poles from where she has her fists planted high on her waist. Ruby's Café sits in a row of old, dark-brick, two-story buildings that make up one side of the road in downtown Chancey. Across the street is the town square, not exactly a square as it's only got roads on two sides of it. One side and most of the other end is railroad tracks and parking. The old railroad depot, now the history museum, is across the square and away from the buildings on Main Street. Several of the Main Street buildings are empty of any business ventures, but full of junk. Occasionally, some of the windows come to life as a shop moves in, then the light goes slowly out as the business dies. Yet, all the while, the café ticks on.

Ruby has no hours listed because she's open when she wants to be open. However, every morning, except Sunday of course, she's here bright and early serving coffee and muffins. No menu, whatever flavor she fixes is what you'll eat. And you'll like it. Then she closes whenever she runs out of muffins or needs to do laundry at home or just gets tired of people. Sometimes she opens at night if there's something going on in town—a football game, election night, or she sees a new pie recipe on Facebook. Then she opens and serves pie and coffee. Again, no schedule, no hours—you're just supposed to know.

Libby, Ruby's one employee, buzzes by with a pot of coffee in one hand, stuffing her pad of order tickets back into the pocket of her apron with the other. "Don't have no cords on microphones no more. Them weather people have them little mics clipped on their clothes. Hey, Carolina," she says on her way by.

Ruby scowls at her, but waves me in with one of her

16

scrawny arms. "When it gets cold this early in the season and starts raining everyone gets all excited that it might snow. It ain't gonna snow this early. Look at that sky."

She takes hold of one of my coat sleeves and pulls me to the front window. "Say, Carolina, what kind of coat is that? It's awfully soft feeling. What'd you pay for that? Buy it down in one of those fancy stores where you used to live?"

I jerk my arm away from her. (Not too hard, it *is* a nice coat.) "It is cold. And I heard from two forecasters that it might snow. Why are you so bothered by it?"

Ruby fans both her hands at me in disgust. "My daughter Jewel signed up to be the coordinator of the calling tree for when they let school out early and somehow I've ended up being the one in charge. Ask me how something like that happens?"

She tips toward the window to look out at the sky again, so she's not expecting an answer to her question. It's just something folks say. She leans back toward me and scowls as she looks around her restaurant. "Reckon most these folks are here for the Christmas meeting? Missus commandeered that long table back there beside the counter before first light this morning. She's directed folks at all those tables in the middle to turn their chairs to face her. If it does start to snow that could be a good thing because if everyone's looking at Missus and her usual dog and pony show, no one will notice it's snowing." She stares at me and demands, "Ain't that right, Carolina?"

"Sure," I say with a quick nod, then I point at her sweatshirt. The shirt is red with an appliqué Christmas tree on the front. "Getting in the Christmas spirit already? Cute sweatshirt."

"Might as well, Jewel gets me a new one for every holiday every year. First few were right cute." She looks down and pulls it out to see better. "This one is from before she had the last kid." There are four big balls hanging on the limbs in bright shades, and stitched on each is a name. She points to each name, then to the empty ball near the top. "This one here was for the baby, but we never got around to putting her name on it. Guess I could do it with a marker, seeing as she's already near five years old."

Libby zips toward us, stopping to refresh a cup of

coffee at the table beside Ruby. "You told me to tell you when that buzzer goes off. Well, it's going off."

Ruby starts off for the back, then turns to me. "Carolina, you keep an eye on that sky. You see one snowflake and you let me know."

I nod and even salute her, but keep walking until I'm at the booth where my friend Laney is seated.

To the untrained eye, Ruby's would appear to have a throwback decor, except it never changed so it *could* be thrown back. The tables have wide edges of shiny chrome and tops with little sparkles in the laminate. Turquoise leather, or something that looks like leather, covers the seats in the booths, while the same material in red and yellow covers the spinning stools at the back counter, which divides the customers from the open kitchen. All that is retro and kind of cool, but the rest is just cheap and old. Blonde paneling, a bathroom opening right off the main room, display cases crammed full of pictures of baseball teams wearing "Ruby's Café" on their shirts. Even inside the display case, the pictures wear a thick layer of dust.

Every table and booth has someone seated at it, and

lots of people are holding seats for others. I'm not sitting up there with folks I don't know to watch for snow, which we all know isn't happening. Besides, not my worry. I didn't sign up for any snow phone tree.

Oh, wait, I think I might've actually. Oh well, someone will call me to tell me if I did, I'm sure. Folks here aren't real good at letting you know what's actually going on, but miss something and everyone becomes Paul Revere. I shake my head and say, "Hey, Laney."

Laney doesn't look up from her phone, but picks up her big, bright blue purse and sits it on the other side of her next to the wall, making a space for me to sit down. I don't know what, but I'm sure the big, shiny, gold logo hanging from her purse means something. Laney only buys things with labels and logos that mean something — mostly that she spent a lot of money. She looks like a beauty queen. Acts like one, too. To be fair, she was actually in the Mrs. Georgia Pageant recently and did well. Still hard for me to believe she's my friend and helps with the B&B. Pretty people usually make me uncomfortable. She directs me with her finger as she says, "Sit down. I'm deciding the theme for Shaw's and my Christmas decorating this year."

Our side of the booth is facing the front windows, so technically I can still keep an eye out for snowflakes. I slide in beside her as I see two purses already sitting on the other bench. "Is that Susan's purse? Who else is sitting here?"

She looks up and across the table. "Oh, yeah, that's Susan's and Momma's."

Susan is Laney's sister. I look around but don't see either woman. "Where are they?"

Laney rolls her eyes, still focusing on her phone. "Missus sent them out to drag Charles down here from the newspaper. Guess he told Momma he wasn't coming since he's on deadline. Momma relayed that message from him to Missus and got sent off like Missus' errand boy." Her perfectly tweezed eyebrows contract in thought. "Think it'd be strange if we did a nautical theme? Anchors and sailboats on the tree? Navy ribbons with gold trim? I've never done that." She looks up, but in a vague way like she's picturing what a nautical theme would mean. She shakes her head and looks back down. "No. It'd be weird up here in the mountains."

I have nothing to add to her Pinterest conversation, so I say, "This place is filling up. Do you know what we're all doing here? Missus said it's a Christmas crisis. What's going on?"

Laney puts her phone upside down on the table. "Where are the muffins? My coffee is getting cold." She waves her hand to catch Libby's eye. Libby nods at us, then moves on around the tables on the other side of the room. Laney huffs and her curled bangs lift with the current of breath. Laney's hair is dark, shiny, and always styled. Big hair may be a joke in some areas of the country, but not in small towns in the south. You know those bumper stickers about "Salt Life" or "Cowboy Life"? Laney should start a line called, "Big Hair Life." She huffs again and this time tosses her head to make her curls bounce a bit. "I can't abide cold coffee. Ruby's especially."

Ruby's coffee isn't anything to write home about, but her muffins are incredible. She is always coming up with new combinations, and from the smells this

22

morning she's moved into Christmas flavors. Peppermint, cinnamon, and some others I can't place, but I've got all month to taste them. Muffins don't have calories, you understand. They're not like those decadent cupcakes. Right?

"I'm here, Missus," hollers a man coming in the front door. Charles Spoon, the editor of the *Chancey Vedette*. "Let's get this meeting started. I'm giving you five minutes." He spreads his hand open to show his five digits, then he plunks down at the front table where a group of young moms scoot over the paraphernalia from their morning coffee. Wonder if they even know there's a meeting? Missus said she'd booked Ruby's just for this meeting, but there wasn't a sign on the door. Maybe the young moms just wandered in by mistake. They aren't really connected with the town. They live in one of the newer, nice subdivisions out by the highway. It's a long drive for folks to work in Atlanta, but I guess they know what they're doing. Charles doesn't excuse himself or apologize. He just flips his notebook open and leans over it with pen ready.

Susan and her mother, Gladys, dart in behind him

and make their way to our table just as Libby comes to fill our coffee cups and bring a basket of fresh muffins.

Missus frowns at Libby, extending her displeasure to our entire table. Missus is tall and thin and actually looks older than she is because she sits in judgement of, well, everything, and that burden shows in her tight gray curls, pursed lips, and stern eyes. Her face usually appears even thinner than it actually is, because she's normally looking down her nose at whatever is in front of her. Right now it's all of us sitting towards the back of the café. With a lift of her nose she includes the rest of her audience in her condemnation. She's an equal-opportunity critic.

"Susan and Gladys, if you ladies can settle yourselves, we will excuse your tardiness and start our meeting. That is, if your table has sufficient food and drink to make it through the next hour. Laney? Carolina?"

A plate of warm muffins arrived for our table at the same time Susan and her mother rushed in to take their place. Laney could've eaten warm muffins for her talent in the Mrs. Georgia pageant because she makes such a show of it. With Missus staring at us, Laney takes a huge bite of a muffin, complete with a moan and indecent facial expressions. Then, her mouth full and her big purple-blue eyes wide, she gives Missus a cheerful thumbs-up.

Laney's mother and sister both hiss at her and tell her to behave as they know Missus isn't above calling a person out, no matter the setting. But public humiliation is not an effective control mechanism for Laney Troutman Conner.

However, it works pretty well for the rest of us as the remainder of the room quiets. We look up at Missus with something she can choose to think of as respect. However, it's mostly the gloves. Missus wears white gloves, and white gloves speak to girls raised in the South. They ask things like, "Where are your manners?", "Must you chew so loudly?", and "Is that really how you were raised?"

A wave of a gloved hand causes Libby to fade back toward the kitchen with her coffee pot—at least our cups got filled—and Missus begins. "Thank you, ladies and gentlemen, for coming this morning to address a crisis in the making for our town. I am confident many, if not most, of you have seen the posters, mailings, and even that atrocious billboard on the highway about Collinswood's Christmas Tree Festival coming up in three weeks."

Cathy Stone, Libby's twenty-five-year-old daughter, exclaims, "It looks amazing! I heard the same folks that do the laser light show out at Stone Mountain are doing Collinswood's Saturday night show. We should get a bus together and go. Maybe we could get a discount!" Cathy met her life's pinnacle as a high school cheerleader, and she's never coming down off that high. She works with the cheerleaders still and maintains that perky spirit at all times. It comes in very handy in her occupation as an at-home lingerie party rep.

The white glove comes up, a tad late, but it does stop Cathy. Missus stares down the cheerleader. "We are *not* participating in that debacle, which Collinswood can only put on due to the fact that they stole our grant money."

"Won it fair and square," Charles Spoon cries out. "I was there at the awarding ceremony just like you, Missus."

Laney sighs loudly. "Collinswood did have a right nice presentation. Don't think we really ever stood a chance." She looks across the table at her sister. "Think we can use the church bus to take a group to the laser show?"

Several speak up that they want to reserve places on the bus before Missus smacks her clipboard against the table she's standing in front of. "No! This is not about any of that. It's about what are we going to do to *compete* with Collinswood. What is Chancey going to offer to visitors for Christmas?"

Ruby comes out from behind the counter and raises her hand. Missus doesn't see her at first, but then Ruby clears her throat loudly. Missus pauses as she looks suspiciously at Ruby. The two women have never been friendly, and Missus is right to be suspicious. Matter of fact, if Ruby raised her hand and it held a gun, that would've been a tad less suspicious.

"Yes, Ruby?"

"I want to say something."

When she doesn't, Missus lifts a gloved hand and

makes a come-on motion. "Yes, we see your raised hand. What do you want to say?"

Ruby lowers her hand, then folds her arms and tucks both hands high under them. "I want to say that, um…" She swallows and takes a deep breath, then her words rush out. "I agree with Missus." She clamps her mouth shut as the rest of us draw in surprised breaths. Including Missus.

With her hands still tucked, Ruby takes a step forward and continues. "We've got to take care that we don't just shrivel up and blow away like some towns do. My Jewel wants to stay here in Chancey, and Lord knows I want them five grandkids to stay here, but look around. Storefronts closing right and left, with the exception of a couple places. *I'm* not going anywhere, but it's a mite depressing to come in here and be one of the only things lit up most days." She turns, untucks her hands, unfolds her arms, and takes a seat at the table beside Missus. All around her we are looking at each other with wide, questioning eyes. This is, this is, well… strange.

Ruby looks up at her nemesis since grade school and says, "What do you have in mind, Missus? I'm all ears."

Now that even makes Laney put her muffin down and pay attention.

CHAPTER 3

Missus swallows and her gloved hands grasp each other, but just as she begins to twist them she catches herself. She's not used to acquiescence. She's used to full pitched battles where she has to demand and manipulate and threaten. However, she recovers quickly, untangles her hands, and presses on the table in front of her with her fingertips. "Thank you, Ruby. Ah, you do have a perspective we, should, uh, listen to and that we, we need."

Now we're all grinning. A humble Missus is as rare as spotting a penguin walking in the square. Our grins get her back in order and she scowls as she says, "However, I don't actually have an actual plan. This all came upon me seeing those awful Collinswood advertisements. There's not time for much of anything *this* Christmas season, but while it's on our minds, we should decide a way forward. Something to build on throughout the next year. Surely everyone can see that? Correct?" Looking at each other we acknowledge she's right. Now is the time to take stock and prepare. Missus watches the bobbing heads around her and continues, "As it stands now, the only community activity we do each year is the Christmas tree lighting. What do we think should be done about that?"

And we're off to the races. Everyone has an opinion now, and the noise rises to fill the big room. The first voices I hear say it's awfully old fashioned and attendance has been down. Many agree with that, and there's talk of something that'll attract young people. "People from Atlanta is who we need!" someone expresses loudly. Last year we were newly moved from Atlanta and I think back to our first Christmas in Chancey. Hard to remember much, it was a pretty hectic month for us, but I do remember the lighting of the tree.

As the voices around me fade, I look up at the old metal decorative ceiling tiles and think about last year's tree lighting. It really was lovely.

In the purple light of dusk the Boy Scouts lit a big bonfire in the far corner of the square. Firelight grew as the sky dimmed and folks approached the square for a cup of apple cider and to greet friends and neighbors. Closer to Main Street, the huge cedar tree was decorated with kid-made decorations, including long construction-paper chains still being made by excited children at a table near Santa Claus' makeshift house. Mr. and Mrs. Claus's thrones sat on a square of old carpet from the depot museum. Their thrones were chairs that I'm pretty sure I'd seen up near the altar of the Presbyterian Church for their minister to sit in. A fake fireplace lit with fake flames accented their painted plywood shack, but as the night grew thicker, magic happened, and it looked as polished as any expensive display at a highfalutin' Atlanta mall.

Bushes at the edges of the square held lots of tiny white lights, and the houses whose old porches faced the square were decked in bows and greenery and even more lights. When the crowd began moving towards the big, dark tree at the appointed hour for the lighting, I found Jackson, tucked my arm in his, and we followed.

The crisp night air made our noses red and let us see our breath. Then the choir director from church stood up front and suggested we sing some more robust songs to get our blood pumping. So we all sang "Rudolph the Red-Nosed Reindeer," "Frosty the Snowman," and "Jingle Bells." He had big signs to help us through the Twelve Days of Christmas, with the twist that we had to do the motions the kids came up with for each of the days. We ended that with laughter and felt quite a bit warmer. Then we sang "Go Tell It on the Mountain" and "Away in a Manger" and others I don't think get sung on many town squares these days.

As the last notes about the baby in the manger faded away, the choir director melted back into the crowd, and everyone stood still as we were plunged into complete darkness. I'd noticed the house lights being turned off as we walked, which made the square feel intimate and close. But now every light in the square—even the streetlights and store lights—went out. At first the only brightness was from the dying embers of the big fire, but no one was alarmed. Everyone waited.

Then I realized everyone was looking up, so I looked up, too, and saw what they were waiting on.

Stars. Stars blanketed the night sky and twinkled in the bare branches of the trees above us. Like a mantle draped over a woman's head, the velvety dark covered us. The longer I looked, more stars peeked out and their twinkle grew brighter. As my eyes adjusted and more stars appeared, some of the twinkling could be attributed to the tears in my eyes. From the sniffles around me, I wasn't the only one who was moved.

Then, when my heart was almost too full, in the midst of the crowd the song "Silent Night" began. We were no longer cold. Worries melted away. There were only stars and friends and peace. When the song ended, there was a little bustling near the tree, and the child selected to push the button that year did their job. The big, dark tree came to life with large, old-fashioned, colorful bulbs surrounded by tin-foil stars and paper chains. Then slowly the other lights around the square joined the tree, and it was even more magical than before.

However, ever since that night, whenever I look up

into the night sky, I remember that all those stars are still there. Always.

"No!" I yell. "No, you can't change the Chancey tree lighting!"

Everyone stares at me. Those with their backs toward me twist around. Apparently the conversation had moved forward without me. Missus turns in my direction and asks, "Care to elaborate, Carolina?"

Across the table Susan and her mother smile and encourage me, so I speak up. "To y'all it might seem old-fashioned or boring, but it's not. At least it's not to folks that don't still live in a small town like this. We don't need to try and outdo Atlanta with laser shows and big, new things. I don't know exactly what that means we *should* do, but…" I shrug. "I don't know."

One of the older ladies seated in a booth towards the front stands up and turns to face the room. In her soft Southern voice she says, "Do y'all remember how we decorated the train station back in the war?" A hush falls over the room and a few heads of white and gray hair nod. "Shall I tell you what I remember? Maybe it will help."

Missus says, "Please, Marigene, do share with us." Then, in the greatest shock of the morning, Missus sits down.

CHAPTER 4

"My brothers left for the war—World War Two, you understand—as did many, many others right there at that very station where we have the museum now. Why, it's been years, simply years, since we've seen a passenger train in Chancey. But during the war, it was quite a busy place. Now you understand I had five brothers, all of fighting age. Then add to that my sisters' beaus who also went to war, so my family alone saw quite a few young men off right there. And even two of my sisters, who worked for the war effort in Washington, D.C."

Her chin tilts up as she recites her family's contributions. She's a short woman, but not due to any sort of stoop. She looks like one of those women you find in a garden on a hot summer afternoon who isn't even breaking a sweat, and still smells of powder. She's wearing a dark-red turtleneck and a brown plaid pantsuit, and her hair has that decidedly blue tint famous among women of her age and beauty shop habits. Her accent is thick and rich, like good homemade eggnog. I could listen to her all day.

"I was the youngest in my family, and so all those goings and comings are a bit jumbled in my memory. Of course some stand out more than others. My sister May coming home from D.C. on a stretcher with the flu. We only had her three days after that. Strange with so many off fighting, she was the first young person in our town to die during the war. When some of the boys did die, those coffins being unloaded right there on the depot platform was heartbreaking." She stops and steps toward the back of the booth near her to put out a steadying hand. With a deep breath she collects herself. "Then my brother Hugh coming home without his leg. Y'all know Hugh, right? Still grows the best tomatoes in Georgia." She laughs as people testify to her claim around the room. Gladys wipes her eyes, and I see others in the café doing the same.

"Oh, but it wasn't all sad. There was the Christmas after the war was over. Christmas 1945. Oh my, we were so happy. And the trains were *so full!* Everybody trying to get home for a peacetime Christmas. My mother cooked and cried and cried and cooked! I don't rightly remember who suggested it, but we wanted our station at Chancey to be the most welcoming station those boys were going to see on their way home!"

Gasps filter around the room as if she'd lit a string of fireworks laying under the tables. "Oh, I do remember that!" "My mamaw always talked about all the lights!" "It made James Arnold get off the train right here and never leave. He married my cousin."

Another older lady who remains seated says, "I actually bought a book about that Christmas written by such a nice young man. Don't remember his name, but it's a fascinating book about how President Roosevelt gave all the federal employees four days off to celebrate. Let me call John and see if he'll bring that book over."

Marigene smiles and waves her hand to get the floor back. "Sounds like a wonderful book. Maybe it'll help us in our planning. That's really all I wanted to say, didn't

CHRISTMAS CRISIS IN *CHANCEY*

mean to ramble on. Sorry about that, but I just think it'd be nice to include the depot in any of our plans."

Missus stands up as the sweet older lady sits down. "Thank you so much, Miss Marigene. That goes right to the top of the list. Yes, Tom? Stand up, if you would."

A man in the middle of the room stands, holding a worn-out ball cap in his hands. "Don't know if this is anything anybody'd be interested it, but since we're talking about trains and Christmas, sure would be good if we could get some interest in a special train ride like some towns do now. Maybe someone with the railroad can look into that. Don't that guy up at that hotel or whatever, don't he work for the railroad?"

As once again everyone turns to look at me, my phone rings. I hold up my phone and say, "I have to get this." Jumping up from my seat, I say hello and dash toward the front door. Luckily the rain has stopped for now. It's the critter catcher guy I left a message with Saturday. I'd put his name in my phone so I wouldn't miss his call.

"Hello, Mrs. Jessup?" he says. "You called about an animal problem?"

"Yes," I say, and try to ignore all the pairs of eyes

staring at me from inside the café. "We have squirrels in our attic apparently, and they're chewing our wires. Least that's what the internet people tell us."

"Ma'am, I can get up there before lunch or so, to take a look around. What's your address now?"

I tell him and he starts going on with memories hunting in the woods by the bridge, but I tune him out while I wait for him to pause so I can find out what time he thinks might be "before lunch or so."

"Can you pinpoint when you might be there?" I ask. "I'm at a meeting downtown and I don't know how long it'll go on."

"That one Missus called? My wife is there, too. When she brings up us needing to have a Christmas parade, you be sure she lets folks know that was my idea. I'll give you a call when I go to head up the hill towards your place, give you a heads-up. Okay?"

"Perfect. Thanks."

"Don't forget about the parade being my idea, you hear?"

"I hear. I better get back in there. Don't want to miss anything."

"Oh, sure thing. Bye."

I open the door and walk back inside. Another gentleman is standing and talking about, uh, he seems to be talking about… cows? At the table, I look at Laney, Susan, and Gladys, but they all just shake their heads and roll their eyes.

Laney leans closer to me. "Murray Glidden. He has a fixation about his cows. You notice Missus hasn't sat down for *him* to talk. We've all discovered if you just let him talk about his cows for a few minutes at whichever meeting he shows up at, he's happy."

Missus claps her hands once and says, "Thank you, Murray. That is good to know, and you are right, those Chick-fil-A cows with those Santa hats on are adorable. I believe we would all be in favor of your cows wearing Santa hats. Next?"

The cow man holds his hand up and leans forward. "Just one more thing, Missus? As I have over thirty cows, that's going to get awfully expensive. Who at the city would I ask about getting some reimbursement?"

Missus's mouth hangs open, and before she can close

it Laney pipes up. "Murray, just check with the mayor. Jed handles all livestock headgear requisitions."

Murray grins, and as he sits down, he says, "Thanks much, Miss Laney. Good to know."

Laughter around the room has Laney preening. Then she says, only partially under her breath, "Jed knew better than to miss this meeting for something silly like taking his kids to Disney World."

CHAPTER 5

One of the young moms at the table where Charles had sat down with his notepad stands up. She has one of those baby carriers on her chest, and we can just glimpse a bit of dark hair on the infant. The woman is attractive, but her voice isn't. I hate to say shrill, but, well, hard? Abrasive? Unforgiving? Her shoulders are set back and her jaw set forward. "What about something that would attract families with children? We moved in over the summer and I guess hearing that there's only *one* Christmas activity is a little disconcerting. The children are our future." She turns to look at the other ladies at her table. Then I notice there is another table of young women and they all seem to be together. They're all nodding. And they look a little angry.

Susan groans, but when I look at her she just closes her eyes and sighs.

Missus says, "Of course children will be welcome at any activity or event. We all—"

"That's copping out," the woman continues. "We're talking about events planned specifically for children. And not just some old man sitting around dressed up like Santa Claus. What about those of us who have chosen to *not* force those lies onto our children about a man coming down the chimney bringing gifts? So far all we've heard is a glorification of soldiers and war and ramblings about the Chick-fil-A cows!"

Susan speaks up, which is good because Missus is not above snatching a person bald-headed. "Athena. Hi," Susan says with a wave of her arm as she sits up on her knees in our booth. (I, for one, am impressed. Heck, I can barely slide in and out of a booth). "Athena, as we've discussed many times at the Lake Park, no one is dissing children in Chancey. Most everyone here has children, and we all love them."

"It wouldn't appear so," the woman, Athena, retorts. "We've yet to find a church with adequate nursery facilities and security. The food choices in this town are abysmal. Just try asking if something is gluten free in *this* place." As her voice raises, her supporters egg her on. "And for anyone truly interested in their child's health, or wanting to eat organic, this town is an absolute nightmare. And while I'm not only addressing *this* establishment, it is horribly offensive to not even try and make your customers happy." She directs her stare at Ruby, who is no longer sitting down and returning the stare.

Tucking a hank of hair behind her ear, Athena implores Ruby with outstretched arms. "How can you *still* not be serving almond milk? Have we not all been asking for it?" The chorus supporting her grows even louder as heads around the room swivel to look at Ruby.

Susan has climbed over her mother and is now standing beside our booth. She holds one arm toward the head table. "Ruby, let me talk to them. Athena, you just moved here. You can't expect things to change overnight."

Ruby squawks. "Susan Troutman Lyles, are you saying *I* should change!? I have absolutely no intention of changing for these stuck-up weenies who don't have the brains God put in a slug. Their manners aren't even fit for slugs."

Missus holds out a gloved hand towards the enraged café owner. "Ruby, you are correct in your evaluation, but please sit back down."

Ruby turns to Missus, ready to unload on her, but then Missus meets her eyes, nods slightly, and winks.

Wait. Missus winked? Only those on this side and behind the two women could've seen it, but that is what it looked like from here. I look to see if the others at my table saw it, but Laney is busy videoing everything on her phone, Gladys appears to be praying, and Susan has moved down the aisle toward the young mothers.

Missus turns back to face the crowd as Ruby sits down. "Athena? I believe that's what Mrs. Lyles called you?"

"Yes." Now Miss Athena may be rude, overly concerned with her child, too thin to have just had a baby (in my opinion), and look too good in yoga pants, but she's apparently not stupid because I can hear the wariness in her voice with just that one word.

"Athena, we appreciate your concern and your ideas, but *you* moved to Chancey. We did not, oh most assuredly we did not, seek you out to move here. Being a bully, albeit a very cute bully, might've worked wherever you came from, but it will not here. You want a better nursery for your little darling? I'm sure there's not a church represented here that doesn't have vacancies on their nursery committee. Am I right?"

Nodding heads and smiles answer her, but she doesn't even pause. "As for almond milk, will it not carry in one of those many metal cups I see sitting there on your table? Those are remarkable for not only their ability to keep things cold but also for their mind-boggling cost, but that is your choice. It is not Ruby's, nor any other vendor in our town's, responsibility to cater to your every silly, narcissistic desire. You need to understand our Christmas celebration will include Santa Claus, flying reindeers, soldiers, cow's milk, and even cows wearing Santa Claus hats giving out Chick-fil-A sandwiches if we so decide. If you want to participate, fine. If your child can't find something to enjoy in all of that, then you're obviously doing a poor job preparing

CHRISTMAS CRISIS IN *Chancey*

your sweetheart for life in the real world. But that's up to you. The people in this room have successfully raised dozens of children—no, scratch that—they've successfully raised dozens of *adults* and do not need your condescending demands. Now, as I always told my son— who went to Harvard, I might add—when he was acting irrationally, you are welcome to stay and participate in this conversation if you can remain civil and act like you have a brain in your head."

At just that moment, Athena's baby wakes up with a start and begins to wail. The young mother looks down and tries to get the baby out of the carrier, but her hands are shaking and then she's crying as hard as the baby. Suddenly she's not the enemy, she's just another overwhelmed, under-rested mom of a new baby. Before her friends can get to her to help, she's surrounded by the grandmothers nearby, and while they can't figure out how to get the carrier unbuckled, they know what to do once the little one is free. One has tucked the baby in her arms and is feeding her from the bottle that was waiting. Athena's sitting down with her head buried in her hands, and Marigene, the lady who talked about her brothers going off to war, has her arms wrapped around her and she's whispering in her ear.

Ruby raises her voice. "Missus, how about a quick break to get some more coffee or go to the bathroom? Libby, hand me my pocketbook."

"Good idea, but where are you going?" Missus asks as Ruby hurries to the front door.

"Running to the Piggly Wiggly. Gonna get some of that almond milk."

CHAPTER 6

There are Southern accents that tickle the ear, lull babies to sleep, and cause the scent of magnolias to float about the room. Then there are Southern accents that cause a reflex squint coupled with a tightening of the mouth. They hurt, no use trying to act like they are cute or homey or bring back good memories. They just hurt. Also, trying to work out the grammar makes you squint even harder.

"My husband? He what wants me to say we should do a parade."

Yes, we are hearing from Mrs. Critter-Getter. She looks over at Athena's group. "Young'uns love a parade, don't they?"

Athena's face is blotched. She tried to leave the meeting after her outburst, but no one would let her.

Even Missus asked her to stay and admitted she'd let her words get away with themselves. That's as close to an apology as we'll ever hear from Missus.

As we refilled our cups and used the restroom, horror stories circled the room about how hard it is to be a new mom. Especially when the young women at the table shared that they had moved here for their husbands or their own jobs and don't have family around. Most of the Chancey ladies expressed their wonder at how you could even raise kids without family to help. You could see that situation had never even crossed most of their minds. I'd raised my kids without family, but I knew I was the odd one in Chancey. In the upscale Atlanta suburbs, no one much had family around. A grandmother who could help out was the exception there, rather than the rule as it is in Chancey.

I think Athena and her friends will find more people applying for fill-in grandma status in the future.

Now, Athena takes a deep breath, looks at Mrs. Critter-Getter, and answers, "Of course. What a wonderful idea!" She smiles around the room, and she gets smiles back. "And Ruby, I'm sorry for making a scene. Thank you for the almond milk."

Ruby just waves a hand at her as she turns toward the back. "No worries. Gotta make a new pot of coffee. Looks like we're in for another round of rain. No snow, but let me tell you, it's getting cold out there."

"Snow?!" The alarm spreads around the room. It's like ringing jingle bells outside a kid's room on Christmas Eve, to say the S-word in a roomful of Southerners.

Missus holds her hand up. "Folks, its forty degrees out there, and it *is* November. It is not going to snow! Now, Arlene, you mentioned a parade?"

"Not me! Chip wants one. Said he went to one down in Atlanta when he was a kid and never forgot it. Said he'd always hankered after being in a parade but ain't never got the chance. Says he'd put together a float of some kind." She throws her hands up. "That's it! All I gotta say!" She sits down. "'Ceptin, hope it don't snow for'n I get home. Mighty good muffins, Miss Ruby!" she yells since our host is back near the oven.

Missus looks across the room. "Thoughts on a parade?"

Laney stands and strikes a pageant pose. She waves at everyone with her queen wave. "As Mrs. Georgia, I was in my share of parades. I must say I'm quite astonished that I never even considered Chancey having one, but we have a perfect setup. Oh, I can see it now..." Her eyes get shiny as she gazes out Ruby's front window.

"It's a chilly Saturday morning," she narrates, "and the street out front is lined with chairs and people. Everyone is holding steaming cups of hot chocolate and coffee. Kids are wearing gloves and hats, and their cheeks are rosy. Those sitting on their daddies' shoulders are bouncing up and down because they see the beginning of the parade coming down the hill from the Methodist church parking lot and turning the corner at the library. Everyone hears the sirens and the band, but all we can see are the flashing lights of the police cars reflecting off everything. Then slowly, so slowly, the police cars creep into sight. The officers in the drivers' seats have their windows down and they are waving.

"In front of the library people are clapping and waving back, then the banner for the high school band turns the corner with two band members holding up the ends of the long pole, proud to lead their friends into the cheering crowds. Behind the banner are the cheerleaders, giving out little footballs and basketballs to the children. The girls in their uniforms are beautiful and healthy and make their mamas' eyes water and their daddies' throats catch. 'Cause of course, every child in the parade has their own audience crowding the street. Then there are the majorettes and the flag carriers leading the band. Oh, how grown up they look! And so serious about their routines, which are done to perfection even as they march forward and pass in front of the row of houses with the old porches. Porches that are overflowing with cheering people. Oh, those porches, like yours, Missus, will be the hottest ticket in town!

"Then the turn onto Main Street, where no cars will be allowed to park, so the path is wide and leaves plenty of room for performing. Oh, those little cars from the Shriners will do circles and honk their horns. There'll be convertibles with the homecoming queen and every girl with a crown we can find. Flatbed trucks loaded with the football team, the soccer teams, the basketball teams, and every team that has enough kids to throw out candy. Ingenious floats with the best backdrops from the drama club, funny floats from the FFA, inspiring floats from the Boy Scouts and the Girl Scouts. The sweet floats from the churches, each with their own blue-draped Mary, a baby, and darling shepherds; cheeks bulging from the Hershey kisses they're supposed to be throwing to the folks.

"Oh, and then the color guard from the VFW will march by and everyone will set their hot chocolate down, stand up, take their hats off, and salute the flag as it's carried by men with white hair who are so proud to be here to carry their flag on a day of celebration. Happy to be here because you can see in their eyes they are thinking of the buddies that never made it back home for a parade.

"Just as folks begin to sit back down, they'll hear it. From the back of a truck with a loudspeaker in its bed they'll hear it. 'Santa Claus is Coming to Town.' All around the truck, which is draped in so much red and green crepe paper it looks like it's floating, elves are walking and handing out candy canes to not only the children, but everyone! The elves look like our neighborhood kids, but surely they came straight from the North Pole, right? Then the shiny, big fire engine comes into view and there, sitting up high next to a fully loaded bag of goodies, is Santa Claus, waving and shouting out, 'Merry Christmas!' Oh, yes, it will be wonderful."

Laney's words stop, but no one seems to notice. We're all staring at the parade going by. Remembering parades of our past. Watching the grandchildren we don't even have yet jump and yell and then go silent when the great man appears. Then slowly we seem to realize the sirens have gone quiet and we're sitting in Ruby's café, not outside on the street.

My friend comes back to herself, blinks a couple times, then slides into the booth beside me. I think she even surprised herself.

"What about breakfast with Santa?" a middle aged lady breaks the silence as she stands up. "Or lunch with Santa. Oh, yes! After the parade we could host lunch with Santa, maybe in the high school gym? All the churches could do it as a fundraiser. At least my daughter's church does it over in Jasper where she lives, and it's always so successful. I can get all the details from her."

Susan twists around in the booth again. "I know we've been looking for some way to join in with the other churches to do a communitywide event. Santa could go from the parade to the lunch. It could be something easy like hot dogs."

Missus nods at Susan. "What if it was only for the children, and parents could drop them off at the lunch for, say, an hour and a half? Then the parents could come back to the square to shop. Maybe some vendor booths in the square and the stores decorated?"

"Oh, I'd love that," one shop owner calls out. "I'd have little treats for the customers. Some hot cider set out for them. Great idea, Missus."

Athena holds her hand up. She's met with smiles, but I can feel that the smiles are a tad tight. Serving the kids hot dogs? Beauty queens? An awful lot of Santa talk — we all wonder what the problem could be now. st

"Yes, Athena?" Missus points at her and tries to smile. Missus trying to smile isn't pretty.

Slowly the young woman stands. She's got a stuffed giraffe in one hand, which she drops on the table as soon as she realizes what she's holding. "Um, me again. Sorry about earlier, my bad. So probably most of you don't know that I'm an interior decorator—well, I used to be. When we lived in Raleigh. That's where we moved from. And, well, one of the things I did was holiday decorating."

Across the table from her, one of her friends yells, "Not just some regular old holiday decorating. She did the governor's mansion. You should see the pictures!"

Charles perks up. "You decorated the governor's

mansion? You say there's pictures? How can I see these pictures? This would make a right nice Christmas article, you know." He starts scribbling on his pad. "Athena, now what's your last name?"

"Oh, it was the company I worked for. Not just me." Athena is actually blushing, and then one of the young ladies at the next table holds up her phone.

"Just google 'North Carolina governor's mansion.' It's stunning!"

As more of us start looking at our phones and thumbing through the images, Athena speaks up. "We didn't do all of that, there were lots of people involved. All I wanted to say was that I'd really like to help decorate. I, uh, that's all." She plops back into her seat.

"That all looks awfully expensive," one gray-haired lady says, and the other three ladies at her table nod in agreement.

"Well, that was for the governor's mansion," another woman says. "They probably have a whole big budget for that."

Athena stands up again. "It wouldn't have to be that expensive. I'm thinking we could use a lot of things from our yards and the woods. I love decorating with magnolia leaves and bark and moss. If we pick a color I can order ribbon for wholesale, or cut up strips of burlap even." She turns toward the windows. "To be honest, I've imagined decorating the gazebo since we moved here."

We crane our necks once again to look outside, across the street at the big, white gazebo. The summer flowers are dead and brown leaves lay in clumps under the benches around its interior railing. The gravel pathways around the park are also obscured by leaves and small branches. Once summer is over, the park doesn't seem to get much attention.

Steadiness grows in Athena's voice. "Boughs of pine, big boughs wired along the railing filled with tiny, soft white lights. The same lights along the inside of the roof so from the outside it appears to glow. Lights on the very top of the roof, to make it look even bigger, regal even. Then I'd hang wreaths of magnolia leaves on the inside and outside of each post so it would look finished from either perspective. I'd line the paths with luminaries, which can be inexpensive if we use milk jugs with their tops cut off and dirt to sit the candles in. They really don't look tacky, despite how they sound," she says with a laugh as she looks around the room. "The only thing I can't figure out is what color to use as an accent. Red ribbon seems so overdone. Burgundy? Gold?"

Missus leans back in her chair as she remembers out loud, "When I was a girl some of the church ladies decorated the old gazebo each Christmas. It wasn't painted white, it was just old gray wood, and of course that was before lights were so inexpensive." She chuckles. "It might've even been before we had electricity in town." The softness around her eyes changes her completely, and I'm not the only one who sees it. Everyone's opinions taper off to let her remember. "Even without the lights, it was magical when the ladies would show up on the square. A wagon full of pine and holly from someone's woods pulled right up to the gazebo, and as the ladies worked the smell would fill the air. Everyone would come out to watch them work. We didn't decorate our house, few people did back then. Oh, some went out and got little trees, but mostly for the kids to decorate with paper chains and popcorn strings. It wasn't like it is today, where everything is so beautifully decorated in our homes. As a girl that gazebo with all the greenery was, well, magical." In the silence of the room, the softness in her face suddenly hardens, and she straightens up. "My father hated it. Decided it was a fire hazard and since he was the mayor, and no one went against him, he stopped it. No more holly. No more pine." She sniffs and looks down at her papers. "I'd forgotten all of that."

The peaceful quiet shifts to an awkward quiet.

Marigene, who'd told of the depot's importance in her family's history, pushes herself up to stand again. "Your father was a hard man. Everyone knew it, but now look at you, bringing Christmas back to Chancey. This is a good thing you're doing, Missus. I remember you as that little girl, and now that you mention it, I remember the decorating of the gazebo. Strange how we've not done it all these years, isn't it? Do you remember that you wore blue almost all the time? You had one white dress that had a rich, blue satin sash with a big bow in the back. Even though I was older than you, I was so envious. How did that bow stay so perfect? I always think of it when I see you."

Missus shrugs. "Blue was my favorite color. Still is, I suppose." She looks down at the blue blouse she has on. "I'm wearing it today."

Marigene laughs. "I thought so. I propose in honor of you bringing Christmas back to Chancey we make blue the accent color for Chancey's Christmas decorations."

Missus gasps, and she's not the only one. We're all so used to fighting her tooth and nail on everything that to honor her feels weird.

Athena, however, claps her hands like a little girl. "Perfect! With all the greenery it will be like the sky. A deep, rich blue." She dips her head and grins. "We'll call it 'Missus Blue.'"

Ruby has left the kitchen and is standing to the side of us. She looks over our table. As longtime Missus foes, she and Laney share scowls, then coordinate an eye roll, but they end with a shrug of whatever. Ruby holds a hand up. "Missus Blue, it is. Okay, now that that's decided, I need some feedback on the muffins.

"Okay, there were chocolate chocolate mint, which

was the dark chocolate ones with the green mint chocolate chips, so there's some color in them. There were the vanilla peppermint ones, and I used crushed candy canes in them. Maybe I should call them vanilla candy cane muffins? The orange cinnamon were the brown ones with the orange bits in them. Could you taste the orange?"

"Oh! Oh!" a lady in the middle of the room shouts. "Oranges! I remember my father talking about how his biggest treat on Christmas morning was receiving an orange. Each of the children got their very own orange."

"Hey, my dad, too!" I say. "Matter of fact, my parents always gave me an orange in my stocking as a reminder."

A gentleman speaks up who hadn't said anything yet. "We each got one at the Christmas party at church. We'd go sing some carols for the shut-ins, come back to the church, and sit in a circle and play games. Then we'd each get an orange, a candy cane, and a little bag of homemade cookies." He grins and slaps his table. "I hadn't thought of that in years. Maybe I'll give an orange to each of the grandkids this year. Good to remember how good we've got it now. Back then that orange was so decadent, such a luxury."

Susan says, "We could add oranges to our decorations in some way, I'm sure. Maybe even dehydrate some slices?"

Ruby says loudly, "Excuse me, but could you taste the orange in the muffins?"

She's answered with a resounding "Yes!"

"Okay, then there were the spice muffins, I thought they looked and tasted a little plain, what'd y'all think?" Around the room there's little enthusiasm and Ruby nods. "That's what I thought."

The gentleman who'd remembered getting an orange at church raises his hand. "Ruby, I was wondering if you've ever made something like a fruitcake muffin. I don't even know if it's possible, but I bet I'm not the only one who would like it. Good fruitcake is hard to come by these days."

Ruby crosses her arms and stares at him—but in a good way. "You know, Harold, my grandmother did make a delicious fruitcake, but nobody in the family kept it up after she died. I'm going to look up that recipe and see what I can do. You'll be my first taste tester!"

When my phone rings, I see it's the critter guy, so I answer it.

"Headed your way, Miss Carolina. That good for you?"

"Sure," I say. "I'll leave right now." I hang up the phone and tuck it in my purse. "I've got to go. Critter guy is on his way." I grab my jacket and duck down to make my way to the front door as the fruitcake conversation continues. (And Lord knows that is one topic that won't ever run out of opinions.) When I push open the door, a blast of cold air hits me, but that's not all.

Snowflakes!

CHAPTER 8

There's a quiet only found in snow. Standing on the sidewalk, I soak it up and watch the flakes fall, muffling the air around me. They make no sound as they drop to the sidewalk and street and instantly melt. Then I hear from inside the café behind me a shout of "It's snowing!", so I quickly move out of the way of the door.

Never mind wearing coats. Snowfall is rare enough here, especially in November, that folks want to stand out in it for a minute.

"Not supposed to lay is what they're saying on my weather app."

"My app doesn't show any snow at all. It's always wrong!"

"Think they'll let school out?"

"Lord, I don't have any groceries at the house."

"My road gets treacherous with ice. Are we supposed to get any ice? I need to get home."

"Reckon I should just go ahead and pick up the kids?"

I'd like to say that everything people say about Southerners losing their minds when it snows is a flat-out, snarky exaggeration by people jealous of our mild winters. However...

It's not. We do kind of lose our minds. But it's mostly in a good way, right?

My phone rings and instantly three people say, "Think that's them calling school off?"

"No, it's my son." I don't add, "Who's at the local college," because they'll think the college is cancelling classes and we would move right in to full-scale panic. "Hi, Will. What's up?"

"My class got cancelled," he says.

Gotta admit, my heart skipped a beat. I exclaim, "For the snow?" Well, that quieted the sidewalk.

"Snow?" he asks. "Is it snowing there? No, professor's sick or something. Anyway, I'm at the house and there's a guy here about the squirrels? Okay if I let him in to check?"

74

"Yes, that'd be great. So I don't need to come home?"

"Hey, look it's snowing here, too!" Will says. "Did you know it was going to snow?"

"No, listen. I'll be home later. You're good there with the critter guy?"

"Sure. Can't believe it's snowing. Think they'll cancel school?"

I growl into the phone, "They better not." Hanging up, I push against the crowd and back into Ruby's. Lots of folks are still in the café talking. Some have their coats on and are leaving. Missus is furiously writing in her notebook while there's a crowd gathered around, talking at her. I hear her say, "I just want to get down as many of the details we discussed as possible."

Laney looks over the heads of some of those standing there and says to me, "Thought you were going home?"

"Will's there. He's handling it."

"Oh my gosh, they cancelled classes at the college?" she exclaims.

Now everyone's talking at *me*.

"No, they did not cancel classes anywhere!" I say, to

nip it in the bud before it can start. "At least as far as I know. It's a flurry. No need to get excited."

However, now the exodus picks up, and a look outside says the snow has picked up, too. It's now hard to see past the gazebo, and I have to admit it makes me nervous. "But I better go on and take care of things at home." Retracing my steps to the front door, Susan joins me and leans close.

She whispers, "Going to the grocery store?"

"Yes," I whisper back. I can't help but sigh and shake my head when I add, "I'm out of bread and milk."

She laughs and says, "Sometimes don't you just feel like you're in a cartoon?" Then she yells, "Hey folks, who wants Chinese for lunch? Let's go up to the buffet. If they call school we'll be close to get the kids, plus, if it keeps up like this there won't be anything left at the Piggly Wiggly. We might as well fill up."

She gets looks of condemnation from several older ladies who consider this a stage one alert to get home and pull up the drawbridge. The tables of younger moms, most of whom have probably lived where snow isn't cause for alarm, all nod and say they'll see her there.

Laney and I look at each other, shrug, and say we're good with it. Missus stands up, picks up her notebooks, and says, "Carolina, I'll ride with you."

Great.

Missus was thrilled when Jackson, I, and our three children moved to Chancey. Not especially about us, per se, more about the possibility she saw in us opening a bed and breakfast. We would provide the only overnight sleeping accommodations in town and overnight sleeping accommodations would nail down her application for a sizeable grant. Or so she thought. Chancey did not win the grant, but here we are—me still taking orders from her. You might've guessed, I'm not real good at saying no.

"Ruby, you coming?" I ask when I realize we're leaving her and Libby with a mess. Missus had mentioned before the meeting that Ruby was hosting the meeting with free muffins and coffee, but we'd reminded everyone to please tip generously. Looking around at the disaster area, I'm sure hoping folks did.

With her hands on her hips, chin jutted to the side, Ruby looks around the room, then says to Libby, "Why not? This'll all be here when we get back, won't it? Libby, I'll drive."

Gladys is pulling on her winter gloves and tsking as she mutters under her breath. Laney walks by her mother and rolls her eyes, so I step up to the older woman. "Anything I can help with, Gladys?"

"All this gallivanting around. I'm still full of muffins, how am I supposed to go eat lunch now? And this Christmas talk just makes me sad. I like our quiet little Christmases here in Chancey. Why does everything always have to be bigger and better? Why can't folks just be happy with how things are?"

"I don't know, but I understand what you're saying. Seems hard to find just the right balance sometimes."

She looks up at me, then turns to look out on the sidewalk where only a few people remain. "Ignore me. I'm just an old woman and I'm tired. We better get out there. Missus will leave without you, even in your car!" She sighs then chuckles, and I follow her out the front door, where Libby waits to lock up behind us.

Libby leans toward Gladys and pats her arm. "Then I'm an old woman, too. I agree with you. Some folks aren't happy unless they have every spare second tied up and written down. But," she shrugs, "we're not the type to stand in the way of other folks' good time, are we?" She and Gladys share another sigh. "See y'all in a minute."

Outside it's still snowing, but not as hard as it was a minute ago. Missus, Laney, and Susan are across the street near our cars. As we join them Susan's voice is raised. "We are not throwing together a parade for this Christmas. Missus, you've lost your mind!"

Gladys says, "Susan!" the way only a mother can say their own child's name.

Susan turns. "Momma. Okay, I'm sorry. But it's just not possible. Not possible. I knew you'd do this, Missus."

"Do what? Try to make our town better. Not wait until God knows when?" She crosses her arms in her gray tweed coat. Her blue blouse picks out the specks of blue in the tweed, and I realize she does wear a lot of blue.

"You mean do a parade now, like this month?" I ask as I click my key fob. With a quick honk of the horn and flash of its lights, we're told my minivan is now unlocked. "I'm with Susan. That's impossible. And crazy."

Missus steps toward my van. "What's crazy is you insisting on locking your car like you still live in the Atlanta area. Chancey is not like it was there."

Gladys speaks up. "Exactly! So why are you all in such a hurry to turn it into Atlanta? Parades, professional decorating, events to keep the kids occupied so the parents can shop. I've changed my mind. I'm not going to lunch with y'all. I've had enough of all this!" She marches carefully over the snow towards her car.

Susan and Laney share a look, then both start after their mother. Missus and I look at each other and share a shrug before we get in the van. We wait for a while, then Laney turns toward us and waves for us to go on, followed by a thumbs-up.

As we pull away, Missus looks over her shoulder at the three Troutman women talking on the sidewalk. "Oh, well," she says. "Sad to see, but Gladys is getting up there, I suppose. Can't let the old people in town hold us back."

I don't even wait for a stop sign to stop the car and stare at her. "Missus! Gladys Trout is your age."

"Not in spirit or energy, apparently. I have always been a very forward-thinking, young-thinking woman. Carolina, why on heaven's earth are you stopped in the middle of the street? Are *you* tired? Should I drive?"

It's my turn to sigh as I let off the brakes and steer forward through the snow. Honestly, at this point I'd rather be looking for squirrel droppings in the attic with Chip the Critter Getter.

CHAPTER 9

And there's the sunshine.

Missus and I had split ways, as I wanted to go into Piggly Wiggly and snag some bread and milk before it was all taken. She went on into the restaurant. I figured it was cold enough for my few groceries to sit in the back of the van while I had a bowl of wonton soup.

Inside the store, there was only mild panic, but by the time I got to the front to check out, sunshine was pouring in the big windows and everyone was breathing a sigh of relief.

"Whew. That was a close one," Cassandra the store clerk says as she scans my items. "Manager was calling in everybody he could find to work. Can you imagine what a snowstorm in November would be like? What a nightmare!"

Cassandra is short, red-headed, and covered in freckles. She's a talker, which is pretty much the only requirement I've identified for cashiers in the south. If you think I'm joking, imagine someone that doesn't like to talk checking you out at a Walmart below the Mason-Dixon Line. Can't do it, can you? They can be big, small, young, old, male, female, incompetent, brilliant, even barefoot—but they must love to talk.

Oh, and ask personal questions.

"I do love a big old snowstorm for snuggling, don't you? Does your husband like to snuggle?" Cassandra asks, holding my huge package of toilet paper over the scanner, running it back and forth. She's talking, so she doesn't notice the barcode is on top. "My boyfriend don't. Gonna be a long, lonely winter, I'm thinking."

Luckily, if you don't jump in with an answer, they most times just talk right on past it. Then bringing all the warmth of the holidays with it, Cassandra is the first, the very first of the season to ask, "You ready for Christmas?"

"It's only November." I couldn't resist. I had to jump in.

"But you don't have any baking items, and it's time to get that started!" She sizes me up. "Unless you're already done. Thought maybe you're one of those people who get things done early. My Aunt Pearl, you know her, she owns the beauty shop, she gets all her shopping done by Halloween at the latest. That's too early in my mind. When do you like to have your shopping done by? That'll be $17.81."

I pay and bag my few groceries since extra help apparently hasn't shown up yet for the snow emergency. I leave without having to answer any of Cassandra's questions, as she's already busy asking the next lady in line about her husband's snuggling routine.

With my groceries in the back of the van and my keys in my hand, just going home sounds like a great idea. Squirrel catcher or wonton soup? It's still pretty cold, and the soup will be hot...

Walking into the restaurant out of the bright sunshine of the now cloudless sky, it takes a moment for my eyes to focus. However, I can hear my group, and as I peek around the fish tank in the middle of the room, I see them.

They've pulled four square tables together in the middle of the room. It's early for lunch, so there's plenty of room. Susan points that she's saved me a space. "I ordered you a bowl of wonton and an iced tea." Thank goodness for good friends.

Before I sit down there's a tug on my sleeve from behind. It's the older woman who mentioned the book about the first Christmas after World War II. "Here, I'm not staying but John brought that book I was telling y'all about. I'll get it back from you at church on Sunday." She hands the book to me and scoots out the door.

People in small towns think you know them. They so rarely have to learn a new face. Plus, everyone *has* always known them their whole life. I don't recall having ever seen this woman before today, and yet she knows what church I go to. Oh well, the others at the table will know who she is. The book is a hardback with a Christmas scene on the front. *Christmas 1945: The Story of the Greatest Celebration in American History.* I flip through a few of the pages on the way to my seat.

"This book looks so interesting. I never knew about this, but it stands to reason with that war over and everyone coming home it would be special," I say as I place the book in Susan's outstretched hand. "How's your mom? I see she didn't come."

Susan sighs. "She's okay, I guess. You don't know, but my dad died at Christmastime. It's been over ten years, but it's still a hard time for her. Of course, she won't admit that. And," she leans toward me as I sit down between her and Laney, "Laney does go a bit overboard with decorating and wanting everything, every little blessed thing, to be perfect. Perfect, expensive decorating, but the activities must be just like when we were growing up."

With a quick peek to make sure her sister is talking to the lady on her other side and not paying attention to us, she continues. "Laney doesn't seem like a very sentimental soul, but when it comes to Christmas, she kind of is. We have to have dinner at Momma's, and every dish has to be the same. Laney's decorating changes every year, but Momma's house has to stay exactly the same. Big, real tree. Same stockings hanging on the fireplace. Same Christmas village on the buffet. We have to open gifts together, all on Christmas morning. The worst thing is she tries to act like it's all for Mom, but it isn't. Mom is very open about not wanting to cook all that food every year. And it's no pain for Laney since Shaw's family lives right here. Plus, Shaw's mom is fine with sharing him and the grandkids. Our brother Scott doesn't have a problem with it since he and Abby Sue are on-again, and he never does anything to help anyway. However, it's a nightmare for me because Griffin's mother feels the same way about Christmas that Laney does—there's only one way to do it, Her Way. *She* wants Christmas morning around *her* tree. With *all* her family. Everyone. Every time. Like they've always done it!"

Susan's hand is white-knuckling the book. Her eyes are wide and she's out of breath as she comes to an abrupt stop. "Oh gosh, I'm sorry. I shouldn't have dumped that on you. Every December it's like this." She realizes her mistake and corrects herself. "Look at me, it's only November. It builds and builds. Hey, here's our soup!" She leans back, lays the book on her lap, covers it with a white cloth napkin, and smiles at me—and her sister on the other side of me—trying to cover up the outburst she just let forth.

Laney smirks at all the whispering and gives us a small eye-roll, but then smiles at Susan and takes a bite of her egg drop soup. Head still tucked towards her bowl, she asks me under her breath, "What's my sister jacked up about now? Please, *please* tell me she is not already starting in on Christmas. She does this every year. And it works out fine every year! She just can't be happy because she's not in control of it. Besides, the kids and Mom would be devastated if we changed even one little bit." She lifts another spoonful of soup and blows on it. "It all doesn't matter one little holly berry to me. Don't know why she gets so worked up."

At this moment, Missus clinks on her water glass and says she's going to read over her notes from the earlier meeting to refresh our minds. I focus on my soup, adding those little fried noodles to my bowl, cutting up the pork-filled wontons, and trying, unsuccessfully, to ignore the memories Laney and Susan have dredged up.

It is apropos, however, that I'm sitting in the middle of them. As the only child, of only children, it's a familiar place to be.

And as uncomfortable as ever.

Chapter 10

"Your mother, my headstrong daughter, found the only Catholic in East Tennessee and married him," my Grandma Jean would say. "Not that I have a problem with Jack being Catholic, but it makes the holidays so very difficult. Why do they have to have a church service on Christmas Eve? And at midnight? Children are supposed to be in bed dreaming about Santa and hearing the reindeer on the roof, not going out and about in the middle of the night. God doesn't care what time you go to church, you know."

My Mimi didn't see it quite that way. "Your Grandma Jean should just wrap the presents under the tree. It wouldn't matter then whether you spent the night under her roof. There's no need to pretend they were just delivered unwrapped out of Santa's sleigh. Some traditions are just silly, I think. It's so simple. Why would you drive all the way across half the state after Midnight Mass, just so you can wake up and pretend Santa Claus brought the presents? Maybe, sweetie, when you were a child, but even then all they had to do was wrap the presents. I don't insist on a full breakfast, just a piece of pastry and cup of coffee, then you'd be driving in the daylight on Christmas morning after a good night's sleep. Just wrap *all* the presents, even the ones from Santa. Doesn't that make sense?"

My grandmothers lived two hours apart, and we lived almost in the middle of them. They were each close to us, but going from one to the other was long enough to actually be a trip. A trip we made every Christmas, sometimes on Christmas Eve and sometimes Christmas Day. My parents did a good job of making sure I was close to all my grandparents, and I loved going to both houses. Warm and welcoming, I don't think either set of my grandparents intended to only have one child, though that was something we didn't talk about back then. They poured everything into their children and seemed to like each other. During the rest of the year,

I didn't feel any of the pull and passion that cropped up at Christmas. However, as I got older, I realized that the parent tug-of-war might have been why my parents bought the houseboat where we spent so many weekends with friends.

But Christmas? Everyone wants to keep their traditions alive, pass them on to the next generation. Dad wanted to go to Midnight Mass, and I did love the candles and being out so late in the dark. There was a connection to the stable, the baby, the animals on those cold nights bundled between my parents, all of us dressed nice and the priest telling the story that never gets old. Dad, and Mom also, wanted to give me that experience every Christmas.

However, that meant that laying in the room where my mother grew up, the room tucked up into my grandparents' roofline with dormer window, pink ruffled curtains back lit with colorful Christmas lights on every window, listening for reindeer hooves and the jingle of bells from my grandfather outside on the deck, had to happen sometime around three a.m.

We had only one night of the year to make it all fit.

And it ALL had to fit. Every single year. When I was little, I thought it was normal. My parents laughed and joked about it, but as I got older there wasn't enough laughter or jokes to cover up their weariness. Then I started complaining, because, that is what kids do, right?

My grandmothers each tried to win me to their side, but I wasn't any different from them. I wanted to have all my traditions, too. I wanted Midnight Mass *and* waking up to find Santa had come and gone.

We talk about kids being greedy at Christmas with their lists and demands. Wonder where they learned *that* from?

Then my grandparents one by one passed away. The houses with all those memories were sold. I went off to college, came home for Christmas, and we had to make completely new traditions. The first year I brought Jackson home on Christmas the power was out! No turkey dinner that day. We actually heated up chili on my parent's kerosene heater and played board games by the light of a hurricane lamp we'd bought my parents as a decoration. So much for traditions, right?

I worried myself silly the first Christmas I spent in Kentucky with Jackson's family. *What would my parents do? Was I ruining their Christmas?* As it turned out, they had some friends over for dinner, went to a movie, and seemed just fine.

By the next Christmas we were engaged and I'd already started wondering how we were going to handle seeing everyone every year since our parents lived far apart.

That year we were all in Kentucky, my parents having been invited up to join Jackson's larger family to celebrate the holiday and our engagement. My mom and dad had driven their new motorhome up and arrived the day after Jackson and I did. We went out to welcome them and help get the RV hooked up since Jackson's parents' house was full. After our tour of their very fancy camper, Jackson and I were getting ready to head inside when my parents said they wanted to speak to us.

"Jackson, it was so nice of your parents to invite us up here for Christmas," my dad said. "Also good to have an excuse to try out our new toy with winter travel."

He laughed and squeezed my mom's waist. They were leaning against the wall in the kitchen area. Jackson and I were still seated on the little mauve couch.

My mom laughed, too. "So far, so good. It was toasty warm last night out at the park. Jackson, I don't know if Carolina's told you, but her Christmases growing up were pretty crazy. My husband and I are both only children, and we just never could make our folks unhappy. They were always so good to us, but Christmas was, well, crazy."

"Sorry, honey," Dad said with a sad look at me.

"No, I agree it was crazy, but…" I shrugged. "I know why you did it and I'm glad you did." I chuckled and added, "Now."

"What we want to tell you both is that you are to never, *never* worry about being with us on any particular day. A birthday, an anniversary, or even Christmas," Dad said.

"*Especially* Christmas," Mom said. "We know we'll see you. We know you love us. We don't need any particular day to make that more true. Okay?"

I jumped up, like young people can jump up from low couches, and hugged them.

"But I *want* to be with you on Christmas," I blurted, but Dad interrupted me.

"And Jackson wants to be with *his* family. Y'all are good kids, good people. But you're making your own family now and you need to think about your own traditions. Your mom and I didn't do that. We just did what we'd always done and ended up having crazy Christmases!"

Mom stroked my hair. "We always said we'd change things when we had another child, but then we didn't get pregnant again and you just made things so easy. That's why we wanted to tell you this now. Don't wait to make these kind of decisions. Life does not get any easier. I promise that! So, think about things now, don't wait."

Jackson was standing behind me now. "I appreciate that, Mr. and Mrs. Butler. I know what you're talking about, my parents decided we would always have Christmas morning in our house. They welcomed everyone to come here, but they were clear they weren't traveling. Might've also had something to do with having three boys who probably weren't as easy as Carolina."

He shook my dad's hand, and my mom reached around him to hug him. Then she stepped down to the door and pushed it open as she said, "We better get inside before they come looking for us."

I followed her, then Jackson came out, my dad last. He closed the door, and we all began across the yard.

"Aren't those icicle lights the prettiest thing?" Mom said. "They just came out this year and seems like they're everywhere, aren't they?"

Surveying Jackson's family's property, my dad asked, "Did your dad get up on a ladder to put them up on the roofline like that? He must be pretty handy, wish I was. Maybe he should write a book about how to do things around the house."

Jackson laughed. "Oh, you should tell him that. He'd love to have a whole new venue to tell people how to do things!"

The Jessups' home sat in a little valley on their old family farm. The outbuildings and pens scattered around the property had lighted stars on them. The hanging icicle lights were on every roofline of the main house, and they were so pretty. Smoke from the fireplace and the woodstove hung in the cold air, and I remember snuggling under my fiancé's arm.

With the wood smoke and animal smells tickling my nose, which was chilled and starting to run, I looked at the home Jackson was raised in. Behind us I could hear my parents talking quietly. As we got closer to the front door, the electric lights even dimmed the sky full of stars. We could hear laughter and music and even the television from inside the warm house.

As Jackson stepped forward to open the door, I rubbed the new ring on my finger with my thumb. I'd already thought of how our love was joining all these people together into something that had never existed before. I'd already thought of that huge thing, but my mother's words now put a new, fairly shocking thought into my head.

Jackson and I were starting our own family. A whole new thing.

My thumb rubs my ring like it did that night. Sitting

here in this Chinese restaurant in a little mountain town in Georgia, the mother of three practically grown children, it's still strange to me how it all happened. And where it's still going.

Chapter 11

"Carolina will help me," Susan says, and that brings me right out of my daydreaming. Shoot, I know better than to let my mind wander around these people.

"I'll help what?"

Susan is holding up the book I'd given her earlier. "Come up with a theme to pull everything together."

Missus sighs. "Carolina, please pay attention. The B&B is critical to our plan. You have our only overnight accommodations. Plus, we are counting on you to help guide us in attracting those living in the Atlanta suburbs. They are our target for tourism."

"Really?" one of the young moms asks as she tucks her shoulder-length hair behind one ear and wrinkles her nose. "Will they *really* drive that far for a small-town parade? I've never lived in Atlanta, but Iici did market research in Lexington for the chamber of commerce and there wasn't a lot of pull away from Lexington for the towns outside their metropolitan area."

Missus just blinks, but I think I can read her mind. It's what I'm thinking. Who are these women with burp cloths on their shoulders, bulky diaper bags at their feet, squalling kids on their laps, but so much knowledge of the world? Athena's experience decorating the governor's mansion, now this one working with the chamber of commerce for a major city.

Why aren't *they* helping Susan come up with a theme?

"Why don't you help Susan come up with a theme?" I ask.

The young woman shrugs. "I'd love to, but we're moving to Houston next week."

The woman next to her gives her a one-armed hug. "We're going to miss you guys so much."

Missus stops blinking and scowls at me. "Carolina, will you just help Susan and stop complaining? It's Christmas whether you like it or not!"

Laney laughs out loud. "There! That's our theme—Christmas, whether you like or not!"

We're all laughing (except for Missus) as our platters of appetizers are delivered to the table. We opted for an assortment to share since we weren't hungry enough for the buffet. We toast the young woman who's moving to Houston with iced tea and water. Missus parcels out assignments and Susan reads us tidbits from the book about Christmas in 1945. However, soon it becomes evident that it's nap time for the babies and toddlers, so that side of the table begins picking up and moving out, taking not only all their baggage, but most of the energy, from the room.

"I have so much to do, I can't believe I'm still sitting here," Susan says. The handful of us around the table echo her.

"My one assignment for the day was to get our internet restored," I say. "We'll see how that goes. And contrary to what I might've told the kids this morning, we *are* having turkey leftovers again tonight, so dinner is done. Wonder if the critter guy is still there?" I pull out my phone and text Will to ask him.

Missus gathers her papers. "I believe we made some real progress on things. That Athena seems to know what she's talking about. She actually drew up a plan while sitting here. Showed it to me before she left. She's going to email it to me along with projected costs." She stands up and puts her coat on. "I'm not exactly sure how I feel about the color blue for Christmas decorations." Her voice is hesitant, which gets our attention. Missus is never hesitant.

The older woman next to her also stands, then reaches out to lay her hand on Missus' sleeve. "It's perfect. Missus Blue ties us to the past and yet makes us look so forward-thinking. No ordinary red and green for us!" She smiles and reaches to pull her coat off the back of her chair. "I'm leaving, too. You ladies ready?"

Her friends agree, and as they make their way to the front counter to pay their parts of the bill, only Susan, Laney, and I are left sitting.

Susan leans forward and lays her arms on the table. I can't help staring at her body-hugging, emerald-green turtleneck. I've always been jealous of how easy skinny people like her make wearing a turtleneck look. There's no mashing of skin at the top of her neck, so she's not constantly tugging it out to let her breathe. She even leaves the tight sleeves down all the way to her hands, not shoved up to her elbows. The resulting effect looks so neat and grownup, which is why I have a whole drawer full of them at home. Just looking at hers gives me a headache and makes me overheat, though, so they'll stay in their drawer. Susan waves a hand in my face to get my attention. "Carolina, are you listening? I know I just said I have a lot to do, but Evergreens opened over the weekend. Y'all want to run out there before school's out?"

Laney bites her lower lip and with bright eyes nods enthusiastically. "I'm game."

"What's Evergreens? Will says the guy is still up in the attic, by the way, but everything is good there."

Susan grins. "Then Evergreens it is! Don't worry, you'll love it."

We stand and Laney says, "Besides, it might help you two come up with a theme. Carolina, you did hear that Missus wants a theme before the town council meeting tomorrow night, right?"

"What? Susan..."

Susan shrugs. "We didn't want those young things

getting all the glory, getting to do all the fun stuff. Right?"

I sigh and let myself pout a bit. "I miss Christmas in the suburbs where no one knew I existed. It's just not easy hiding in a small town."

CHAPTER 12

"Wait, I have groceries in the van," I say as we walk out the restaurant door.

Susan wraps her arms tight around her. "It's so cold out here. Let's ride together, your groceries will be fine sitting here. I'm assuming you don't have anything frozen?"

"Nope. Eggs and milk are the only things that need to be cold."

Laney presses a button on her keychain and her SUV starts up. "Gotta love remote start when it's cold."

Susan and I just shrug at each other, then Susan opens the back door and directs me to sit up front. Climbing in the back seat, she says to her sister, "You're the one who sleeps with the owner of a car dealership."

"Shaw does come in pretty handy at times," Laney responds, adding a wink.

"How cold do you think it is?" I ask as I shiver in my soft but not very thick coat. "Oh, this does feel good," I add as I settle into the warmth of the car. "And smells good. Must be nice always having that new car smell. So what's this evergreen place we're going to?"

Susan answers. "It's out of town on the old highway. You've been there in the summer, I'm sure. Green's Watermelons? And they sell other stuff, too. Mostly things they grow."

"Oh, the farm stand if you take the backroads to Walmart?"

"Yeah, that's it." Susan talks from the back seat as she thumbs through her phone. "The Green family started it years ago, but it was always empty in the winter. Then one of the sons tried to start a Christmas tree farm years ago, but he got tired of it before the growing part really came together. However, his wife and mother had opened a Christmas shop in the building, and it really took off. They sell all these cute handmade things for Christmas, and the area women work there. I mean, they don't exactly work there, they... oh, you'll see. But now the family sells Christmas trees they ship in, and it works for them."

Laney looks in her rearview mirror at her sister. "So how was Thanksgiving at Griffin's mom's?"

Susan rolls her eyes and puts her phone down. "Awful, as usual. You'd think as wonderful as she thinks her four children are, she'd give her grandchildren a break. She rides them constantly and Griffin and his siblings let her. We in-laws spent our time soothing our kids' feelings and growling with each other about her. Jenny, Griffin's youngest brother's wife, took their two little girls and left early. Left her husband there! Of course, it practically put my mother-in-law in the hospital, or so she said. She could barely lift her hand to eat another chocolate from the Whitman sampler she keeps beside her chair!"

Laney laughs and says to me, "She eats chocolates and doesn't share with the grandchildren, can you imagine? My sister is a saint to put up with her, but even worse is how Griffin and his brothers and sister act. They think their mother can do no wrong. I've never seen a woman able to keep such control over her children."

I twist in my seat to better see Susan. "Griffin's father passed away, right?"

"Yes, when Griffin was nine. She did have a hard life raising the four kids on her own, but come on, she was a bank teller. She wasn't scrubbing toilets or collecting garbage. Anyway, we survived another holiday. What did y'all do?"

Straightening up in my seat I look out the window. "Nothing much. My folks are out west camping. They had their Thanksgiving meal at a lodge in Yellowstone and the pictures looked amazing. Jackson's family were all busy. He and his brothers seem to go their own way for the holidays. I made a much too big turkey and the five of us mostly ate, played games, and watched movies."

The quiet in the car grows to the point that I notice it. "What? What is it?" I ask as I watch Laney and Susan make eye contact in the rearview mirror.

Laney gives me a one-shoulder shrug. "Just never

thought about not having family around. Seems kind of lonely. Kind of weird."

"Not weird," Susan interjects. "Just different. Honestly, though, I can't imagine it either. But you know, those moms at the meeting today. None of them are from around here. They must do the same thing, like y'all do."

"Guys, it's really not that sad. You both look like you're going to start crying!"

We all laugh, and I try to explain. "It's just how it is. And in other places, like when we lived nearer Atlanta, it's not that unusual. There virtually everyone goes away for the actual holidays, especially Christmas and Thanksgiving. If you stay, there are folks left in town who are also looking for something to do. I do have to admit it's different here. Everything pretty much shuts down because you're all together. But it's nice spending time with just us. Really quiet and calm."

"We should've invited you over," Laney says.

"No, no. It really is okay. We have our own traditions, and then some years we have company or we go to our parents' houses."

The quietness descends again, and just as I think I need to try and explain better, Laney says, "We're here. Oh look, there's Momma's car. I thought she might've come out here after the meeting."

We climb out of the big SUV, and along with the cold, I'm hit with pine scent. Trees are everywhere, not in the ground, but in piles and in stands. Wood smoke from the chimney mingles with the smoke from a small fire to the side.

"Hey, Chuck," Susan calls as she waves. "I see you've got daytime duty."

The young man stands from his seat on a log beside the fire, his hands never leaving his jean pockets. "Yes, ma'am. Y'all need a tree today?"

Laney and Susan both shake their heads. "Nope. One night this week with the kids we're thinking," Laney says.

"Us, too. Chuck, this is our friend Carolina Jessup. She and her husband own the B&B up by the bridge."

He nods to me. "Nice to meet you, ma'am. Y'all got that place of yours looking good. My youngest loves to go up the bridge and watch trains. We were up there just last week. But you ladies better get inside quick, this cold'll cut you right in two. Supposed to warm up tomorrow, but you know we'll still have the hot chocolate ready. Merry Christmas to you and yours!"

Turning to look past the trees, the happy little fire, and the red-cheeked young man, I survey the red clay hills that lead to dense woods, still with some brightly colored leaves on a few trees. Most, however, are bare, and I can see the birds flitting in and out as they work over the harvested cornfield. I take a deep breath and smile. "Now this is how you should get a Christmas tree."

My friends agree. Then as Laney reaches to pull open the heavy front door of the bare wooden building she asks me, "So where do y'all usually get your tree?"

My smile is bit lopsided as I say, "Home Depot."

And I thought they felt sorry for me before.

CHAPTER 13

"So I hear you girls are trying to outdo Mr. Disney for Christmas right here in our little town." This is how we're greeted, by an older lady with a mass of gray curls held back with a candy-cane striped headband. She has on a crochet vest with little jingle bells stitched into the yarn, and I can't help but grin as she walks towards us.

Behind her is a fireplace. Around the fire, all seated in rocking chairs, are a half dozen ladies around Mrs. Troutman's age. There are a couple much older and a couple much younger. They are all crocheting or knitting or sewing, everyone doing some kind of handcraft.

Laney whispers to her sister from the side of her mouth, "Look, someone belled the cat." Then she steps forward all smiles and sugarplums, "Why, Mrs. Green, no way we would even *try* to outdo Mr. Disney. Have you seen that Cinderella's castle done up with all those lights? Oh my, our little town couldn't afford that light bill for even one night! We are actually thinking of honoring the Christmas of 1945 and thought we'd come here to get *your* memories of that year since it was sooo long ago."

Susan and I both take a small step back. I've heard a lightning strike can travel through the floor to those standing nearby.

The woman's bells ring as she raises both arms, then flings them outward as if to shoo Laney away. She turns to go back to the circle of ladies sitting near the fireplace.

"Wilma, you're exaggerating what I said, and Laney, you're just being ugly. Stop it and apologize," Mrs. Troutman says to her daughter—and apparently to Mrs. Green—as they both obey her orders.

As we step closer to the ladies, Susan whispers to me from behind her hand. "Momma and Wilma Green have been best friends since they were in kindergarten, maybe before." Then she pulls me forward. "Hey y'all, this is Carolina Jessup. She runs the bed and breakfast up on the hill. I know some of you have met her."

"Susan," Mrs. Greens says, "there's a crockpot of mulled cider over there if you want some. And the coffee is right fresh. Carolina, you've come by here in the summer, haven't you?"

"Yes, I have. We ate a record number of watermelons this year. Yours are so delicious. I didn't know you sold Christmas trees."

Laney laments, "They get their tree at Home Depot."

Great, now everybody feels sorry for us. "We haven't lived here that long," I defend my family's honor. "This year we will be coming out here. So, are you ladies making the crafts to sell?"

"Yes," answers a lady near me with unnaturally red hair swept up in a beauty shop hairdo. "First it was just for fun, a way to get together and visit. Then once they started selling Christmas trees, we decided to sell things, too, to raise money to give Christmas to a needy family in the area." Her voice is low and rough, but it rises as she says, "Last year we gave food and gifts to four families. Four! Just our little group of women making stuff."

"Well, I can't wait to look at everything. Nice to meet

y'all." I turn to the back wall where there are shelves packed with their handiwork. Susan meets me there with a Styrofoam cup of cider.

"I always find teachers' gifts here for the kids to give. Plus everyone knows what the money goes for, so folks enjoy receiving gifts from here. Oh, look at these little quilted drink coasters! They have herbs in them that smell nice when you sit a warm cup on them." Susan's mom calls to her, so she walks away from me toward the fire, where Laney has sat down in an empty rocking chair.

A scarf the color of Savannah's eyes is my first purchasing decision. Then I find two more: one that will be perfect for my mother and one for Jackson's mother that has jingle bells on the fringe. She's the type that likes jingle bells. When I see a rack of vests like the festive one Mrs. Green is wearing, I go to them, but none are large enough for Etta. Picking one up, I walk to the circle. Maybe they can make a larger one.

"So you weren't joking about the Christmas of 1945?" Wilma is asking Laney. The older woman's face is closed and cold.

Laney's head tilts in a question as she says, "No, I wasn't joking, but I was mean. Sorry about that."

Mrs. Green smiles and her face relaxes a bit. "Actually it's the year I was born. While I don't remember anything, it was a pretty big Christmas in my family."

Laney's mom sharply inhales, and her hand flies to cover her mouth. "Oh, Wilma. I'd forgotten about that."

With soft sigh and a tiny smile, Wilma excuses her lifelong friend. She settles back in her chair and laces her fingers in her lap. "It was the end of the war, and my mother went all the way to Savannah on the train to meet my father that Christmas. The plan was for it to be a reunion for them since they'd been apart for so long. Christmas in Savannah, just the two of them. I got left with my grandparents on my first Christmas."

"So your father was coming home from the war like all those others?" Susan's face lights up as she says, "You're the first person we've talked to with this actual story, like in the book we're looking at."

Wilma reaches up and runs her fingers through her mop of gray curls as she looks away from Susan, then stares into the fire. "I suppose. Except, except he never came home. He'd asked my mother to meet him in Savannah not to celebrate, like they all thought, but to tell her he was leaving us. He said he couldn't come home and face everyone in Chancey, but he owed it to her to tell her to her face. Folks back here didn't know that, of course. Everyone went down to the station to welcome them home, but it was just my mother that got off the train. Alone. We never saw him again, even for my grandparents' funerals. I never met my father."

Laney goes over to Wilma's chair and kneels down in front of her. "Oh, Miss Wilma, I didn't know. I'm so sorry. I should've never said all that. You poor thing." She pets the older woman's hand.

Wilma grasps Laney's hand. "Thank you, sugar. You didn't know. Not sure anyone here but your momma knew all that."

Gladys Troutman shakes her head and smiles at her friend.

With her crochet yarn twisted around her fingers, the red-haired lady says, "Of course I knew your daddy was gone, but I kind of thought he died in the war."

Others around the group nod and agree that that's what they'd thought.

Wilma sighs. "We pretty much acted like that, too. There were so many people grieving, I guess it all just kinda rolled into one. Plus, all those soldiers coming home, things were probably confusing enough. Matter of fact, I grew up thinking he died in the war because it just wasn't something we talked about, but when I got older my mother told me the truth." She breathes deeply and releases it slowly as her chest deflates. Then she smiles looking around her. "But that's why I love celebrating Christmas now. My mother hated everything to do with Christmas the whole time I was growing up. She only did what she had to to keep folks from talking, until"—she reaches over and pats the knee of the younger woman sitting beside her—"until I started having the kids. Then it was like every Christmas thing she'd skipped, every bit of fun she'd denied herself and us around her, she was going to enjoy."

The woman next to her grins. "Granny loved Christmas. I didn't know the whole story until I was grown and having my own kids." She looks up at me and Susan standing next to each other. "What a fitting tribute to celebrate that Christmas again in Chancey. Count me in to help."

Gladys speaks up. "What we were discussing before you girls came in is that we don't want some fancy light show and tourist trap events like some towns around here do." Around the circle heads nod and I find myself nodding along with them.

I turn and look at the bare-bones building. Pine and yarn and warm fabrics. Winter-white knitted mittens and stuffed ornaments made of black and red flannel. The aroma of cider and coffee mingle with the smell of melted wax from the candles in the window. Everything is softened through the haze of smoke from the fire in the room, and I shift to look at it and those seated around it. Some of these ladies gathered here have known each other longer than I've been alive. They knew about each other's children before those babies were given names. They know the heartaches that gave their friends a touch of sadness around the edges of their lives. They know the joys that made them able to give joy to their families, their homes, their town.

"This," I say. "This is what folks need. To be with people who know them. To be included, to be pulled to their place beside the fire. I fought tooth and nail to keep from moving here, and yet I see this is where I needed to be all along. Especially at Christmas."

Susan reaches for my hand and squeezes it. "Now, to put all that in a theme."

There goes my good mood.

Chapter 14

I let Susan ride shotgun on the way home. "I'm worn out," I say as I lay my head back and take a deep breath of the leather headrest in Laney's back seat. "It's been an exhausting day."

"Are you getting heat back there?" Susan asks me, then shifts towards her sister. "I'm surprised Momma never told us about Miss Wilma's father, aren't you?"

Laney pulls out onto the highway. "I think she honestly forgot. Maybe this whole dredging up the past thing isn't such a good idea. Too emotional for the holidays."

"Oh, you're always like that," Susan says. "Just fun and laughing, that's all you ever want. Of course with a snide comment here and there."

"Better than rushing around trying to make everything

CHRISTMAS CRISIS IN *CHANCEY*

mean something. Can't we just have a simple parade? Everything else is fine just like it is. Right, Carolina?" Laney looks for my approval in the rearview mirror.

I shrug, saying, "This sounds like a family issue. I'm staying out of it."

"It is not a family issue," Susan insists. "At least not just our family. Those young moms today, and families like yours who don't have ties here, you need a connection. Do we really want to just be all surface, all flash at Christmas?" Susan's voice raises even more. "Like the ladies at Evergreens were saying, all lights and hoopla?"

There's a pause and then I start giggling and laughter explodes from Laney. "Hoopla? Hoopla? There's our theme – No Hoopla!"

Susan's long, tanned face breaks into a big smile as she rolls her eyes. "Okay, scratch hoopla. But y'all know what I mean." She shifts further in her seat to look at both me and her sister. "Christmas Connections, or Connecting at Christmas, or... I don't know. C'mon, Carolina, you're supposed to be helping with this theme thing."

"Critter guy is still at the house," I say looking up from my phone. "Savannah and Bryan will be home from school soon. Don't you hate how dark it gets this time of year? I'll think about the theme after dinner, I promise."

Laney groans. "Dinner. Wonder what I'm fixing tonight. Those people I live with always seem to be hungry."

I agree. "My mom used to say she didn't mind cooking dinner, but she hated coming up with what to fix every night. Used to be I didn't understand, but I do now. Gets to this time of day and I know somebody is supposed to be fixing something to eat, then I remember it's me." I end with a long sigh.

In the waning afternoon light we ride along the backroads of North Georgia in silence. The clouds have thickened again but without dropping any precipitation, thank goodness. My mind wanders around the day, the meeting at Ruby's, getting to know the younger moms at lunch, Missus Blue, Evergreens, and how good it felt to just be there, hearing Wilma Green's story. "Wonder if she knows what happened to her father?"

Apparently my friends' minds were wandering the same paths. Susan doesn't skip a beat. "Yeah. How strange would that be? Never knowing when he might just pop back into town."

Laney says, "Sure makes you understand her mother hating Christmas. But then to make such a turnaround to loving it! You know, I remember her, Wilma's mother. She was just another grandma in my mind." As she pulls into the Piggly Wiggly parking lot where Susan's and my vehicles are, she sighs. "You just never know, do you? What other people are going through or have lived through."

Susan puts her hand on Laney's arm. "That's all I was saying earlier. Or trying to say. It'd be so great if we could find a way to make Christmas in Chancey help people feel like they can let down their guard. They can rest and have fun. Oh, I don't know. Anyway, thanks for driving."

Laney puts the car in park and turns off the engine. "I'm going in the Piggly Wiggly to see what I can find easy for supper."

I laugh. "The tireder I get, the better that leftover

turkey sounds. And I know 'tireder' isn't a word, but it should be."

Laney stretches as she steps out of the tall SUV, then shouts at her sister, already at her own car, "Hey, what are you fixing for supper?"

Susan turns back towards us, her ponytail swinging. With her jeggings, no makeup, and the energy that is practically visible as it rolls off her, she looks more like the mom of one of the toddlers from this morning than a mom of teenagers. "Oh, I have a pork roast and veggies in the crockpot." She smiles and shrugs at us, then jumps into her car.

Some people just make life hard, you know?

Chapter 15

School buses are pulling up in front of the middle and high schools, so I hurry to get on the road before them. As I turn up the hill towards home, I flip on the radio and hear the first Christmas carol of the season. Now with CDs and downloaded music you can listen to carols all year long, but I smile, remembering how we'd listen with the kids for that first carol that never played before Thanksgiving. Never.

At the top of the hill, the road curves along the bluff with the river down below on my left. Just past the curve, our drive cuts off to the left through all the head-high weeds that are now brown and dead. Even with my windows up, radio on, and heater blowing, I can hear the horn of an oncoming train crossing the tall bridge.

We get steady railroad traffic, hence the appeal of a

131

railfan bed and breakfast here. I stop and watch as the tons of steel roar past me. The ribbon of cars following the huge engines winds down the mountain on the other side of the river and across the bridge. Our house sat empty for a long time before we came along. Most people probably thought having a busy train track crossing your driveway would be less than ideal. Oh, and then there was the ghost thing—but that's another story for another day.

Anyway, it was like this house sitting high above the river in this tiny mountain town was waiting for us. As the last railroad car flies past me, I pull the van out of park and ease across the tracks. Chip, the critter guy, is waiting on the porch.

"Hey, Miss Carolina!" he says. "That was some awful long meeting y'all been at. Did my wife mention the parade? She say it was my idea?"

"She sure did," I say as I exit my car with groceries in tow. "And I've been doing some other errands, although the meeting did go on quite a while. So what about the attic?"

He meets me down on the sidewalk. "Got ya all

set. Closed up the hole I found, then had some metal screening I put up so they shouldn't be able to get past it. I also set a trap, so I'll be back to check that. Did some straightening of stuff up there to make it easier to work around in your attic. Y'all might want to look at adding some insulation up there once we get this squirrel situation finalized. Looked a mite skimpy on insulation. I know a guy that can do that if the mister don't feel like doing it."

I set my bags of groceries on the top step and pull my pocketbook open. "Can I write you a check?"

"Oh, no, ma'am. I mean a check is fine, but don't pay me. My wife handles all the business stuff. One too many checks got put through the washer 'cause I'd just stuff 'em in my pants pockets, so she took over all billing. She'll write out and send you a bill some time. No hurry."

"Well, thank you. I guess now I just need to get the internet people out to fix that."

"No, ma'am. I went ahead and fixed that up for ya. Just needed to repair a couple wires. Electronics stuff like that is kind of a hobby with me. Plus, I figured there's no need for you to have to keep waiting and pay for them to come out."

As he's talking, Savannah and Bryan pull across the tracks and into the driveway. I wave at them, but quickly turn my attention back to him and say, "Really? That's awful nice. My kids will be thrilled."

Chip grins. "Well, we're neighbors, you know. Gotta look out for each other."

Huh, well whaddaya know? Now I have a "guy."

We watch as Savannah and Bryan collect their books from the car's back seat. Late afternoon sunshine pierces the clouds and bathes us in orange light with a purple tinge. In the shaft of light we suddenly see tiny crystalized snowflakes dancing in the air around us. The kids' faces light up. Chip turns, looking all around. The air is full of light and tiny flakes, and the kids can barely walk for turning in their own circles. All of our mouths hang open in smiles of awe.

Savannah says breathlessly, "It's like being in a snow globe."

"That it is," Chip says, then he bends to pick up his toolbox. After another look around, he starts down the sidewalk, saying over his shoulder, "Nice to meet you, Mrs. Jessup. You can call me anytime!" As they pass on the sidewalk, he says, "Welcome home, kids." Then he turns around, walking backwards, surveying us and our home. "Sure is a good place to come home to."

And just like that, I have our theme for Christmas in Chancey.

Chancey: A Good Place to Come Home To.

The End & Merry Christmas

If you've enjoyed this quick visit to Chancey, be sure to read the first book in the series, *Next Stop, Chancey.* (You can find the first chapter of *Next Stop, Chancey* at the end of this book.) All my books are available on Amazon, in both e-book and print versions. Signed copies are available, too! Just look on my website: www.KayDewShostak.com. You can also say hello to me on Facebook and on Instagram and Twitter at @ KayDewShostak.

And as the Welcome to Chancey sign says, "Holler if you need anything!"

The book about Christmas 1945 is a real book! When I began researching Christmas pasts in the South, especially with a connection to the railroads, articles from the book *Christmas 1945: The Story of the Greatest Celebration in American History* by Matthew Litt showed up. I ordered the book and found it just wonderful. The subtitle is *The Story of the Greatest Celebration in American History* and it was published in 2010 by History Publishing Company. If like me, you collect Christmas books, this would be a great addition.

Here is the first chapter of the first book in the Chancey series.

Enjoy!

CHAPTER 1

So how did I get stuck driving with my daughter, the princess, during one of her moods? Rap music, to pacify her, adds to my sense of disbelief. Carolina Jessup, you have lost your mind thinking this move can work.

Rolling hills of dry, green grass and swooping curves of blacktop lead us to a four-way stop. Across the road, sitting caddy-corner, is the sign I found so adorable last October. When we still owned a home in the Atlanta suburbs and moving hadn't entered the picture.

"Welcome to Chancey, Georgia. Holler if you need anything!"

A scream of "Help!" jumps to my lips, but that might disturb her highness. Maybe she's asleep and won't see her new hometown's welcome.

"Holler? Who says 'holler'? Who puts it on their sign for everyone to see?"

Nope, she saw it.

With a grimace, my voice rises above Snoop Dog, or whoever is filling my car with cringe-inducing music, as we cross the highway. "Honey, it's different from home, but we'll get used to it, right? And Daddy's really happy. Don't you think he's happy?" She dismisses my question, and me, by closing her eyes and laying her head back.

I stick my tongue out at the sign as we pass. I hate small towns.

Savannah sighs and plants her feet on the dashboard, "All my friends back home want me to stay with them on weekends." Drumming manicured fingernails on the door handle of my minivan she adds, "Nobody can believe you did this to me."

Guilt causes my throat to tighten. "Honestly, Savannah, I'm having trouble believing it, too." Apparently, she's tired of my apologizing because she leans forward and turns up the radio. Rap music now pounds down Chancey's main street, but no one turns an evil eye on our small caravan. Two o'clock on a Sunday afternoon, there's no one to notice our arrival. July heat has driven everyone off the front porches, into air conditioned living rooms. Bikes and skateboards lie discarded in several yards, owners abandoning them for less strenuous activity, like fudgesicles and Uno.

Jackson is driving the rental truck ahead of my van in which our twenty years of life together are packed tighter than the traffic at home. Oh, yeah, Atlanta isn't home anymore. As the truck takes a curve, I have a view inside the cab. With their grins and high fives, they might as well be sitting on the driving seat of a Conestoga wagon headed into the Wild West. Next to Jackson in the truck is our thirteen-year-old, Bryan. Beside the passenger window is our older son, Will. Bryan is ecstatic about this move. Will just wants to get it done so he can get back to his apartment at the University of Georgia.

We slow to take a turn where two little boys in faded jeans lean against the stop sign post. After Jackson passes, the taller one steps toward the road and waves. I press the brake pedal harder and roll down the window.

Humidity and the buzz of bugs from the weeds in the roadside ditch roll in.

"Hey guys."

"You moving here?" He punctuates his question with a toss of his head toward the moving truck lumbering on down the road ahead of us.

"Sure are. I'm Carolina and this is Savannah."

The smaller boy twists the front of his red-clay-stained t-shirt in his hands and steps closer. "Ask 'em."

"I am," the speaker for the pair growls as he shoves his hand out to maintain his distance from the younger boy. "You moving up to the house by the bridge?"

"The train bridge?"

He nods and both boys' eyes grow larger. They lean toward me.

"Yes, you can come visit when we get settled."

Both boys shake their heads and the designated speaker drawls, "No, ma'am. Can't." He pulls a ball cap out of his back pocket and tips his head down to put it on.

The little one keeps shaking his head and finally asks, "Ain't you afraid?"

Savannah moans beside me, "Mom..."

"No, we like trains. Well, we'd better be going."

"You ain't afraid of the ghost?"

My foot jumps off the accelerator and finds the brake pedal. My finger leaves off rolling up my window. "What?"

But they don't hear me. The boys are running toward the house sitting in the yard full of weeds.

Savannah grins for the first time today. "Did he say 'ghost'? Cool." She turns the music back up, lays her head against the head-rest and we pull away from the corner.

Ghost? Like there's not enough to worry about.

Tiny yards of sunbaked grass and red dirt pass on the left. Across from them a string of small concrete buildings house a laundromat, a fabric store, and Jeans-R-Us. Chancey's version of an open-air shopping mall. Hopefully, Savannah's eyes are closed as I speed up to catch the truck. Over a small hill, the truck comes into view along with a railroad crossing. A smile pushes through my worries as I think of the grin surely on my husband's face right now.

For years, Jackson talked about moving and opening a bed & breakfast for railroad enthusiasts, railfans, in some little town. Now, a lot of people fantasize about living in a small town. I believe those are the people who have never lived in one—like my husband.

Only five weeks ago, he came home with a job offer from the railroad. We'd already experienced life with the railroad in our early married life. When we finally tired of his constant traveling, he took a job with an engineering consultant and we moved to the upscale suburbs northwest of Atlanta. Railroad job, or no, nothing was getting me out of the suburbs.

Then I find condoms in Savannah's purse, freak out, and accidentally make his dream come true. Well, the small town part of his dream, but the B&B is not happening. Things won't get out of hand again, not with me focusing.

At the railroad underpass there is no stop sign or light, but Jackson and the boys are stopped anyway. Arms poke out of both windows of the truck cab. There's no train coming but Bryan and Will spent more father-son outings in rail yards than parks so they could be pointing at one of a hundred things of interest.

At first Jackson's train obsession was cute, but I realize now, I'm an enabler. Like the husband walking down his basement stairs when it dawns on him his den could double as a scrap-booking store. Or the wife suddenly realizing her last ten vacations involved a NASCAR event.

Past the railroad yard and up the hill overlooking town, the harsh sunlight is muted by thick, leafy boughs drooped over the street. Shade allows for thick lawns encased behind wrought-iron fences or old-stone borders. Sidewalks cut through the lawns and lead to deep front porches and tall houses. The houses stand as a testament to Chancey's once high hopes—hopes centered on the railroad and the river. As we come to the top of the summit the River runs on our right. Savannah leans forward to look out her window, pushing her dark hair back. Ahh, even she can't ignore the view.

"Mom, you realize we are officially in the middle of nowhere, right? Look, nothing but trees and water as far as you can see. Not even a boat in all that water. I guess everybody's inside watching *The Antiques Roadshow*."

So much for enjoying the view. We turn away from the river and start back down the hill, taking a sharp turn to our right. A narrow road maneuvers through a green channel of head-high weeds. The road and weeds end in wide-open sky and a three-track crossing.

"Great, a stupid train already," Savannah growls. We can't see the train but up ahead her father and brothers are out of the truck and pointing down the line. We both know what that means.

I put the van into park and lay my head on the steering wheel. My sense of disbelief wars with the memory of the joy on my husband's face. Is it possible for us to be happy here? A train whistle blows as dark blue engines rock past and my head jerks up. Through the blur of rushing train cars I see the other side of the tracks—and our new home.

Frustration cuts through my sadness because someone is sitting on the front porch. Are you kidding me? A drop-in visitor already?

To Continue Reading, Find This Book on Amazon

The Chancey Series

Next Stop, Chancey
Book One

Looking in your teenage daughter's purse is never a good idea.

After all, it ended up with Carolina opening a B&B for railroad buffs in a
tiny Georgia mountain town. Carolina knows all about, and hates, small
towns. How did she end up leaving her wonderful Atlanta suburbs behind
while making her husband's dreams come true?

Unlike back home in the suburbs with privacy fences and automatic
garage doors, everybody in Chancey thinks your business is their business
and they all love the newest Chancey business. The B&B hosts a senate
candidate, a tea for the County Fair beauty contestants, and railroad nuts
who sit out by the tracks and record the sound of a train going by. Yet,
nobody believes Carolina prefers the 'burbs.

Oh, yeah, and if you just ignore a ghost, will it go away?

Chancey Family Lies
Book Two

Holidays are different in small towns. You're expected to cook.

Carolina is determined her first holiday season as a
stay-at-home mom will be perfect. However...

Twelve kids from college (and one nobody seems to know)
Eleven chili dinners (why do we always have to feed a crowd?)
Ten dozen fake birds (cardinals, no less)
Nine hours without power (but lots of stranded guests)
Eight angry council members (wait, where's the town's money?)
Seven trains a-blowin' (all the time. All. The. Time.)
Six weeks with relatives (six weeks?!?)
Five plotting teens (again, who is that girl?)
Four in-laws staying (and staying, and staying...)
Three dogs a-barking (who brought the dogs?)
Two big ol' secrets (and they ain't wrapped in ribbons
under the tree, either)
And the perfect season gone with the wind.

Derailed in Chancey
Book Three

Should she jump?

When the train is headed for disaster, the engineer can jump out, right?

Carolina knew moving teenagers from the Atlanta suburbs to a small Georgia mountain town was a horrible idea. She knew opening a B&B was an even worse plan. She can't see around the next curve, but...

Should she jump?

Oncoming headlights aren't only aimed at her family, the town of Chancey is being set up for a collision that could change everything. And as that unfolds, Carolina's husband Jackson is smack dab in the middle of it all, his hand on the throttle, going full steam ahead.

Should she jump?

Would you?

Chancey Jobs
Book Four

Aren't small towns
supposed to be boring?

Overnight, a shiny new business opens on Chancey, Georgia's Main Street, with a manager straight from New York City who doesn't find the South charming, at all. Carolina's bookstore is also opening on Main Street. *If* she can keep Patty's mind on books instead of a new romance.

Then, when a secret wedding catches everyone off guard, a springtime tornado in Chancey just seems like icing on the cake. (Wedding cake, that is.)

Trains still run by Crossings, the B&B for rail road enthusiasts. Ruby still sells coffee and muffins. And kids still get out of school for the summer.

However, even in a small town, change is constant.

New jobs mean a move for long-time Chancey residents. Cancelled plans lead to moves across the state—and broken hearts. Graduations mean new chapters. And babies mean…well…

Babies mean nothing will ever be the same again.

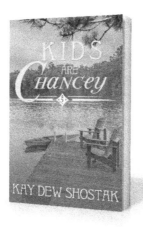

Kids Are Chancey
Book Five

"A mother is only as happy
as her unhappiest child," they say.
But is it true?

What if your children are all miserable, Carolina wonders, but your life is finally coming together?

Will's new marriage and new job, are already old. Savannah's reduced to chasing a guy and she's playing the Southern Belle to do it. Bryan is labeled a stalker. Maybe worse, is he a world-class liar?

Carolina's friends are having kid worries, too. Laney's finding the age gap between high school senior and newborn grows with her exhaustion. Susan's kids too quickly get accustomed, and attached, to their new station in life in their ritzy mountain community. Missus schemes to have her great-grandchild living under her roof, but that means living with a pregnant teenager first.

Why *do* people keep having kids?

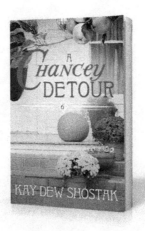

A Chancey Detour
Book Six

*Aren't detours supposed to have
big warning signs?*

So why do life's detours come out of the blue and hit so hard?

It's been a year since they opened the Bed & Breakfast for Railfans
in the small town of Chancey and the Jessups feel as if they've always lived in the Georgia Mountains. After a hard summer, Carolina
is looking forward to the cooler temperatures of autumn and the
routine of the school year. However...

Unplanned detours mean more family in town, families pulling
apart at the seams, and just plain ol' heartache.

Unplanned detours mean moonshine, chocolate pie, and blue ging-
ham on the town square.

Unplanned detours mean sleepless nights, sweet surprises, and hesitant hope.

Unplanned detours mean, well, they mean life.

CPSIA information can be obtained
at www.ICGtesting.com
Printed in the USA
FSHW020720311019
63547FS